A Problem for Mother Christmas

A Problem For Mother Christmas

Ted Willis

Illustrated by Jill Bennett

LONDON
VICTOR GOLLANCZ LTD
1986

First published in Great Britain 1986
by Victor Gollancz Ltd,
14 Henrietta Street, London WC2E 8QJ

British Library Cataloguing in Publication Data
Willis, Ted
   A problem for Mother Christmas.
   I. Title
   823′.912[J]   PZ7

   ISBN 0-575-03884-5

Photoset in Great Britain by
Rowland Phototypesetting Ltd, Bury St Edmunds, Suffolk
and printed by St Edmundsbury Press Ltd,
Bury St Edmunds, Suffolk

For The Mob (my grandchildren)
and for my friend, Tup Wayland

1

Two or three years ago, about two months after Christmas, the man in charge of the Post Office sent for Postman Fred Hale. Fred worked down below in the basement where he helped to sort the thousands and thousands of letters that come in every day. Most of these letters were fed into a special machine which could read the postcode on each envelope, and then direct the letters to their proper destination.

But, of course, there were many letters which did not have the postcode on them, or were addressed to the wrong place, or on which the handwriting was so bad that it was quite impossible even to read the address. It was Fred's job to deal with these difficult letters. Officially, Fred's department was called the Department for the Handling of Incorrectly Addressed Mail, but this was far too big and

7

clumsy for Fred and his mates. They simply called it the Department for Wonky Letters.

Some Wonky Letters were easy to deal with. Quite a number came in addressed to Popeye the Sailor or to Donald Duck and similar characters, and Fred simply sent these on to Hollywood film studios in the United States. Other Wonky Letters were a little more difficult and some were quite hard.

Once a letter came in addressed to: Sergeant Wilkins, Royal Engineers, Fort Stanley. Fred thought about this for a few moments and then realised that the address should have been *Port* Stanley. So, off the letter went to Sergeant Wilkins in the Falkland Islands, who was very pleased to get it because it was from a friend who owed him £7.50 and there was a cheque in the envelope.

Part of Fred's job was to look after the letters which came in addressed to Father Christmas. There were hundreds and hundreds of these every year. A lot came in before Christmas Day, from children who were writing to ask Father Christmas to bring them a special present. And a lot came in after Christmas, mostly from children who wished to thank him for bringing their presents (although there were a few who wrote to complain that they

had not got the present they had asked for).

All these letters were put into a big box marked: Father Christmas—Lapland, near the North Pole. When there were enough to fill a large sack, a special postman called William would take the sack on a helicopter and drop it by parachute in the back garden of Father Christmas's house.

Fred was pondering over an especially Wonky Letter when the very important person upstairs sent for him. Fred was a very determined man— some people might have called him stubborn—and it was his proud boast that no Wonky Letter had ever defeated him.

But this one was really difficult. It was addressed, in rather bad joined-up writing, to: H.M.O., Pal Mal, London. Fred decided that the very important person upstairs would have to wait while he solved this sticky problem.

He turned the letter over and over in his hands. He stared at the address for the hundredth time: H.M.O., Pal Mal, London. Whatever could it mean? He opened the drawer of his desk, took out a powerful magnifying glass and examined the envelope again.

"Ho," he muttered to himself, "what is this?"

Underneath the O he saw, or he thought he saw,

the tiniest little squiggle. He studied it for a long time. Yes, there was no doubt about it. There *was* a little squiggle attached to the O, just at the bottom. Underneath the magnifying glass it looked like this:

Q

It was not the letter O at all. It was Q. And the address was really H.M.Q., Pal Mal, London. In a flash, the answer came to Fred. H.M.Q. could only mean Her Majesty the Queen. Pal Mal, of course, was all wrong. Whoever had sent the letter should have put The Mall, for that is the wide road which leads to Buckingham Palace.

With a smile of satisfaction, Fred wrote the proper address on the envelope:

> Her Majesty the Queen,
> Buckingham Palace,
> The Mall,
> London

He dropped it into the special box which was reserved for Royal Letters. Then, after washing his hands and combing his hair, he got into the lift and went up to see the very important person.

The very important person, Mr Ulysses B Smedley (his name was painted on his office door), frowned at Fred when he arrived.

"You took your time," he said.

"Pardon?" said Fred politely. He was not really listening. It was the first time he had ever been in Mr Smedley's office and he was fascinated by the view. Through the window behind the large desk he could see halfway across London; he could see St Paul's Cathedral surrounded by the tall buildings of the City.

And the office itself was quite splendid. It was so big that Fred reckoned he could fit his own kitchen, the parlour and Beth's bedroom into it, and still have some room left over.

It had a beautiful, thick gold-coloured carpet, some armchairs to match and, along one side, a dark polished table with ten chairs round it. Mr Smedley's desk was huge and shining and the chair in which he sat was like a throne. Fred counted five telephones on the desk, a sure sign that Mr Smedley was very important indeed.

"A nice place you have here," said Fred.

"What was that?" snapped Mr Smedley. He was a very busy man—or at least he thought he was—and like all busy men he was inclined to be irritable and snappy.

"A nice place," said Fred, with a smile. And, because he was anxious to get back to the Wonky Letters, he added: "Well, I have things to do if you haven't. What is it you want?"

Mr Smedley was not at all used to being spoken to in this blunt way, especially by a postman, and he frowned again.

"It so happens that I have a great deal of work on hand," he snapped. "I am a very busy man."

Fred could not help but notice that, apart from

the five telephones, the big desk was empty. Not a piece of paper in sight. Not a single letter! It didn't look to him as if Mr Smedley was busy. But he kept this thought to himself and simply said:

"Well, I'll take your word for it."

"Let us get on, please!" said Mr Smedley. "I believe you handle the letters that are addressed to Father Christmas?"

"That's right," said Fred, who was looking out of the window again and wondering if it would be possible to walk to St Paul's across the rooftops.

"And how many have we got so far?" asked Mr Smedley.

"Five thousand, two hundred and twenty-three thank you letters, and one thousand, six hundred and fourteen thank you postcards," answered Fred promptly. He had counted them only the day before and he had a very good memory.

"I think it is time they were delivered," said Mr Smedley.

"If you say so," said Fred. "I'll bundle them up and give them to William."

"William," said Mr Smedley, "William has retired."

"Oh," said Fred, tearing his eyes away from the view. Postman William had been delivering letters

to Father Christmas for years and it came as something of a shock to hear that he would no longer be
doing it.

"The letters must be delivered," said Mr Smedley.

"Quite right," said Fred. "Absolutely."

"By a Qualified Postman," said Mr Smedley.

"Wouldn't do to put them in the hands of an
Unqualified Postman," agreed Fred.

"That is why we want you to take them," said
Mr Smedley. He sat back in the big chair, put his
finger-tips together, and smiled. It wasn't much of
a smile, for Mr Smedley did not smile very often
and he was out of practise, but the muscles of his
face moved and a little gleam came into his eyes. He
obviously expected Fred to be pleased by the news.

Fred scratched his head with one hand and
stroked his chin with the other. It was difficult, but
he had got into the habit of doing so whenever he
was faced with a problem.

"It is a sort of promotion," said Mr Smedley,
who was still trying to smile. "And you will receive
an increase in wages of £1.00 per week."

"Very nice," said Fred. "All the same, I can't do
it."

"And why not?" snapped Mr Smedley, giving up

the attempt to smile.

"I could not leave Beth," said Fred.

"Beth?" Mr Smedley frowned. He felt much more comfortable when he was frowning.

"My daughter. I can't leave Beth on her own," said Fred.

Mr Smedley was about to ask about Beth's mother, but he remembered just in time that Fred was a widower. Fred's wife had died in an accident six years before.

There was a little silence, and then Mr Smedley said: "Why not take your daughter with you?"

"Take her with me!" said Fred, who was rather shocked by the suggestion. "Take Beth with me on a helicopter, all the way to Lapland! All that snow and ice!"

"You don't have to stay," said Mr Smedley. "You know the procedure. You simply fly over Father Christmas's house and drop the letters by parachute into his garden. Then you come home. It

17

will make a very nice trip for her. I'm sure she will
enjoy a ride in our helicopter."

"I don't know about that," said Fred doubtfully.

"It will be an adventure for her," said Mr Smedley.

"I don't know about that," Fred repeated.

"You know the motto of the Post Office?" said
Mr Smedley. The snap had quite gone from his
voice now.

Fred knew the motto by heart. He said:

> Come sleet or rain, come hail or snow,
> The letters and parcels have to go.

"So you see," said Mr Smedley, "it is your
duty."

"Yes," said Fred. He put his shoulders back.
"Very well. I'll do it."

"Good man!" said Mr Smedley. His smile
looked almost real this time.

And that was how it all began.

2

Beth Hale had a strange prickly sense of excitement as she left school that afternoon. Of course, she didn't yet know about her father's conversation with Mr Smedley but she was sure—or almost sure— that something thrilling was about to happen, an adventure in which she would be involved.

If you had asked her about it, she would have found it very difficult to explain. It was just a— well—a *feeling*. Ever since she could remember, these feelings had come to her from time to time and they nearly always turned out to be true.

For instance, about eighteen months before, she had woken up one Saturday morning with one of her feelings. She told her father about it at breakfast, but he had simply poured some more milk over his cornflakes and smiled.

"We have to clean this place from top to bottom

this morning," he said. "That is the only excitement we are likely to see today."

Beth always helped Fred to clean the house on Saturday mornings. She quite liked whooshing over the carpets with the vacuum cleaner, but it wasn't what she would call really exciting.

"No," she said. "We shall have to leave cleaning the house until tomorrow. I am sure that something thrilling is going to happen today. I feel it in my bones."

Beth was not quite sure what feeling things in your bones meant, but she had heard her father use the expression and it exactly fitted the way she felt. The sense that something exciting was about to happen seemed to be tingling and prickling her whole body.

But Fred just said, "We shall just have to see", and filled his mouth with cornflakes. Beth loved her father, but he did have an infuriating way of saying "We shall just have to see" at critical moments. She wondered sometimes if he used the words simply because he could think of nothing else to say.

On that particular morning, however, they had hardly finished their breakfast when the doorbell rang. Lo and behold, who should be on the doorstep, smiling from ear to ear, but Beth's favourite uncle, Dan! He was a short, rather plump man with a face as rosy and shiny as a ripe plum, and hair as white as a clean handkerchief.

Dan lived in Canada where he had a very successful business making sausages and meat pies and all sorts of cakes. But here he was, on their doorstep, announcing in his booming voice that he had come to Britain on a surprise holiday; he had a car outside and he was going to take them both to the seaside for the day.

Well, *that* was what Beth called exciting. No doubt about it. And when, six months later, she had another one of her feelings, and told her father that something thrilling was about to happen, Fred did not dismiss the idea with "We shall just have to see". He still did not quite believe her, but she noticed that he kept looking out of the window to see if Uncle Dan had turned up again.

But, on this occasion, the surprise had arrived by post. A letter came for Beth to say that she had won second prize in a newspaper competition for the best poem by a child under the age of nine. The prize was two free tickets for a performance of *Treasure Island* at the Old Vic Theatre, after which Beth would be allowed to go backstage and meet the actors.

Naturally, after this, Fred began to have more respect for Beth's 'feelings', although he did not tell her. So he was only slightly surprised when, on the Saturday morning after his meeting with Mr Smedley, Beth said:

"Daddy, I think something exciting is going to happen."

"Oh," said Fred, "what makes you think that?"

"I just have a feeling," said Beth.

Fred smiled to himself. This time he knew more about it than she did and he decided to tease her just a little.

"Oh yes, my lass," he said, "something exciting is going to happen tonight."

"You see! I knew it!" said Beth, her eyes shining. "What is it, Daddy?"

They were eating their breakfast in the kitchen and Fred very slowly spooned up some cornflakes, put them into his mouth and chewed for a half-minute before replying. Beth couldn't eat. She waited anxiously for his reply.

"We are not going to have supper at home tonight," Fred said at last. "I am going to take you to the Sunset Hamburger Bar in the High Street."

Beth liked going to the Sunset, but it was hardly

22

what she thought of as an adventure. The disappointment showed on her face.

"Oh," she said, in a small voice.

"I shall buy you a Sunset Special Whopper Hamburger with chips, and a coke, and ice cream to follow," said Fred, continuing to tease her.

The Special Whopper was Beth's favourite and she adored ice cream, especially if it was vanilla and strawberry mixed and had little flakes of nuts on top, but she was still disappointed.

"I was thinking of something much more exciting than that," she said.

Fred looked at her long face and smiled. He decided that he had teased her enough. "There is something else," he said.

"What is it? What is it?" asked Beth, perking up again.

Fred rose from his chair and began to collect the plates from the table. "Let's clear these things away," he said, "then we'll take Battersea for a walk on the common. I'll tell you all about it then."

Battersea was a little white Scots terrier that Fred had bought from the Dogs' Home. He was about six months old when an inspector from the Royal Society for the Prevention of Cruelty to

Animals found him, half-starving and frightened, by the side of a motorway and took him to the Home where there were hundreds of other home-less dogs.

He attached himself to Beth in more ways than one when they first met, for he jumped up at her, his tail wagging like a flag in a strong wind, and fastened his white teeth into the sleeve of her school

25

blazer. She tried to make him let go, but he refused. It was as if he were saying: I've found you, I like you, and I am not going to let you go.

So she picked him up in her arms and he promptly licked her face. Fred watched this with his slow smile and said: "We came here to choose a dog—but it looks to me as if that dog has chosen you!"

"I think he is beautiful," Beth said, hugging the little terrier.

"Has he got a name?" Fred asked the young lady keeper.

"Not at the moment," she replied. "Only a number. 25637."

"We can't call him that!" said Beth firmly. "25637. He's a dog, not a telephone number!" Her eye fell on the sign of the Home. "Battersea!" she said.

"Battersea?" asked Fred.

"That's what we will call him," said Beth.

"A very good name, too," said the young lady keeper.

And Battersea barked as if to say that he liked his new name much better than his old number.

He was a very affectionate and intelligent dog and he soon learned to respond, not only to his

name, but to other words too, like 'Come' and 'Sit'
and 'Lie Down'.

One of his very favourite words was 'Walk' and,
when he heard Fred talk about a walk on the
common, he jumped up from the rug on which he
had been lying and began to bark.

"Whoops!" Fred said, "I've done it again! I
should know better than to say W-A-L-K in front of
that animal. He knows exactly what it means." He
patted the dog and quietened him down. "All right,
boy. Go and get your lead."

Battersea trotted off and came back a moment or
so later with the lead in his mouth, his tail wagging
nineteen to the dozen and his bright eyes shining
with enthusiasm. Fred put on his heavy overcoat,
Beth put on her anorak with the red hood, and they
set off.

When they reached the common, Battersea was
released from the lead and he went running off in
wide circles as if he were chasing invisible rabbits.
As they watched him, Fred told Beth all about his
conversation with Mr Smedley, his new job and the
visit they had to make to Father Christmas.

It was as much as Beth could do to stop herself
turning cartwheels on the wet grass, she was so
excited.

27

"I knew it!" she cried, "I knew it! I knew something thrilling was going to happen!" And she hugged her father in sheer joy.

"Steady on," Fred said gruffly, "steady on. I've got a Mars bar in my pocket and you will squash it!"

They sat on a seat under a huge plane tree and shared the Mars bar, and talked about their great new adventure.

"What is it like in a helicopter?" asked Beth.

"Noisy, I should imagine," said Fred, "very noisy."

"And how long will we be away?"

"Four or five days," Fred replied. "Maybe a week—you're lucky that you are on half term from school."

"Very lucky," said Beth, and sighed happily.

Just at this moment, Battersea came trotting back to them with a piece of an old tree branch in his mouth. He laid this down at Beth's feet and looked at her proudly, as if to say: Look, I've brought you a nice present.

A sudden thought struck Beth and she turned to her father.

"What about Battersea?"

"What about him?" asked Fred.

28

"I can't leave Battersea for a whole week!"

Battersea barked in agreement.

"Quiet!" said Fred to the dog, and turned to Beth.

"We can leave him with Mrs Watts. She always takes care of Battersea while you are at school and I'm at my work."

"Mrs Watts is going away to Scotland next week. She will be away for a whole month."

"Ho," said Fred thoughtfully, "that does present a problem."

"I can't leave him," said Beth. She felt sick with disappointment.

"Of course you can't," said Fred. "No more can I. And what is more, I can't leave you. Yes, we do have a problem."

He scratched his head with one hand and stroked his chin with the other. Beth watched him anxiously. Then he stood up suddenly: "Well, there is only one thing for it. We'll take him with us!"

"Take him?" cried Beth.

"Why not? If Mr Smedley doesn't like it, he can find someone else to do the job. Yes, we'll all go."

Once again, Battersea barked in agreement.

"You see!" said Beth. "He likes the idea!"

"And so he should," said her father. "So he

29

should. It is not every day that a dog gets a ride in a helicopter!"

Fred paused for a moment, then he went on in a low voice: "There is one other thing you must remember, Beth. What we are going on is a Special Secret Mission. You must not tell a soul."

"Oh," said Beth. She was disappointed because she had been looking forward to telling her friends all about this grand new adventure.

"If anyone asks, you say that you are going to Norway. You won't be telling a fib—because that is where we go first of all."

"Why must it be a secret?" asked Beth.

"Because there are people," said Fred darkly, "people who would give a million pounds to find out where Father Christmas lives."

Beth was puzzled by all this, but Fred would say no more.

The day passed in a sort of dream. Beth could still hardly believe that she was actually going on a helicopter, actually going to visit Father Christmas.

That night, in bed, she made up a little poem in her head:

A Problem for Mother Christmas

We're all going to Lapland,
Going across the sea
Taking letters to Father Christmas,
Battersea, father and me.

She wanted to make up some more, but she found it very hard to think of a word to rhyme with helicopter. She was still trying to find one when her eyes closed and she fell asleep.

3

A lot of people have the idea that Lapland is flat, as flat as the surface of a snooker table, only white instead of green. It is white very often because it is quite near the North Pole and is covered in snow for many months of the year, but it is certainly not flat.

Beth found this out when she went to the library on the following Monday and looked it up in an atlas. She discovered Lapland in the Arctic Circle and her first surprise was to see how big it was. It stretched for hundreds and hundreds of miles, right across the top of Norway, Sweden and Finland and even across a little bit of Russia.

What is more, she saw from the colours of the map that Lapland was full of high mountains, and hills and valleys and lakes. She examined the map very carefully to see if she could find any clue as to where Father Christmas lived. Was there a place called Christmas Town? Or a village named Santa Claus Village?

She could find nothing whatsoever. But when she spoke to her father about it that evening, he was not at all surprised.

"Didn't I tell you it was a secret?" he said. "Didn't I say that there are a lot of people who would give a fortune to find out where Father Christmas lives? They would organise tours and things and, before you knew it, there would be so many tourists that the reindeers would be killed in the crush! That is why you can't find the place on the map."

"So how will we find his house?" asked Beth.

"The pilot," said Fred. "The pilot of the helicopter. Just before we take off, he will be given Sealed Orders."

"Sealed Orders?"

"An envelope," said Fred. He lowered his voice to a whisper, although no one else was present. "A special sealed envelope. Inside that envelope there will be a secret map showing the valley where Father Christmas lives."

"Do you know where it is?" Beth interrupted.

"Of course not!" Fred snorted. "Even Mr Smedley doesn't know—and he is a very important

33

person. Even the Prime Minister does not know. And I don't believe the Queen knows either."

"If you don't know where it is, how do you know that he lives in a valley?" asked Beth.

"Ho," said Fred, "we are sharp tonight, aren't we! Sharp as a new razor blade!"

"I only asked," said Beth mildly.

"Well, clever-socks," replied her father, "if you must know I made a deduction."

"A deduction?"

"I worked it out. I mean, it stands to reason. Father Christmas could not live on the top of a blooming great mountain, could he? It would not be practical. For a start, it would be too cold and windy."

Beth had to agree that her father was right, but she was a persistent girl and she said: "If you don't know where Father Christmas lives, and if Mr Smedley doesn't know, and the Queen doesn't know, who does? Who gives the pilot of the helicopter those Sealed Orders?"

Fred held a finger to the side of his nose. "That is also Top Secret," he said mysteriously.

"A secret within a secret!" said Beth.

"That is one way of looking at it," said Fred. "Right. That's enough questions for one evening.

We leave in the morning and we have packing to do, arrangements to make. So let us get on."

"Did you speak to Mr Smedley about Battersea?" asked Beth anxiously.

"I did," said Fred, and put on a sad face.

"What did he say?" Beth didn't like her father's gloomy look one little bit.

"Well," said Fred, and hesitated. "Well," he said again, and then his face brightened. "Mr Smedley said it will be all right, providing we don't expect the Post Office to buy Battersea's biscuits for the journey."

"Great!" said Beth, clapping her hands. "But I do wish you wouldn't tease me quite so much!"

Fred had bought Beth a brand-new suitcase and she packed this with some of her warmest clothes. Battersea lay on the rug beside her bed watching her. He did not take his eyes away from her face for one single moment. It was as if he knew that she was going away and he was wondering if he was going to be left behind.

Beth stopped to reassure him. "It's all right, Battersea. You are coming with us." And she tickled him just between the ears. He liked this a lot, and he rolled over so that she could tickle him on the tummy, which he liked even better.

This made her think that perhaps he might be cold in Lapland, even in a helicopter. So, when she had finished packing, she found an old scarf and made him a little jacket which went round his body and buttoned at one side.

It took her quite a time but when it was finished it fitted perfectly. Battersea seemed to be very proud of it, for he ran up and down the stairs a dozen times, wagging his tail and barking.

Fred was a methodical man, and he made out a list of things to be done and pinned it up on the Reminder Board which hung in the kitchen. As each item was dealt with, he ticked it off on the list.

A Problem for Mother Christmas

He wasn't sure quite how long they would be away, so he wrote notes to the milkman and the paperboy asking them not to deliver any milk or newspapers until further notice. Fred checked to see that his passport was in order, as he had not used it since he and Beth went to Benidorm in Spain for a holiday. He checked the aeroplane tickets which Mr Smedley had given him, for they had to fly from London Airport to a place called Oslo first of all, then from Oslo to a town named Senja in the very north of Norway where the helicopter would be waiting for them.

And he checked the Letter of Authority that Mr Smedley had given him. It was typed on official Post Office paper and it read:

To Whom It May Concern

Be it known that Fred Hale is a Qualified Postman. He is hereby authorised to deliver all cards and letters to Father Christmas.

He will be accompanied by his daughter, Beth, and her dog, Battersea. Because of the great importance of this mission, Battersea has been given special exemption from the Law of Quarantine.

Ulysses B Smedley

Ulysses B Smedley
Chief Supervisor

"What does that last bit mean?" asked Beth.

"All dogs coming into Britain are bound by law to spend six months in special government kennels," said Fred. "This is to stop pets bringing diseases into the country. But, for this one special occasion, they are not going to apply the rule to Battersea."

"Thank goodness for that!" said Beth, giving Battersea a big hug. "I couldn't bear to be parted from him for six whole months!"

At last, it seemed that everything was done. Fred said that he would turn off the gas, the electricity and the water in the morning before they left.

"Well, my girl," he said, "I think we are just about ready to go. So I propose that we have a nice cup of hot chocolate and a game of Snakes and Ladders, and then go to bed. Agreed?"

"Agreed," said Beth.

As they were playing the game and sipping their chocolate, Beth suddenly thought of something that would rhyme with 'helicopter'.

She made up another little poem in her head:

Beth climbed on the big helicopter
When a man in a uniform stopped her.
He picked her up by her feet,
Held her over a seat,
And then, with a smile, he just dropped her.

She repeated it to herself. It was quite good, she thought, and quite funny. She imagined herself landing on the seat upside down and smiled.

"What are you smiling at?" asked Fred.

"Oh, nothing," said Beth. She was quite shy about her poetry.

"Well, my girl," said Fred, "you will be smiling on the other side of your face in a minute. You have just thrown a five, which means you will have to go to the top of this very long snake and go right back to the bottom of the board!"

It wasn't Beth's night. Her father won all three games of Snakes and Ladders. But she didn't really mind. She was thinking of the great adventure that was to begin tomorrow, thinking that it was the most exciting thing that had ever happened to her.

4

Of course, there was a hitch. When you have an adventure, something is bound to go wrong. Perhaps that is what makes an adventure more exciting than the things that happen on an ordinary day.

The journey to Oslo, which is the capital city of Norway, went smoothly. The stewardess on the aeroplane was kind to Beth and even took her up to the flight deck to meet the Captain and his co-pilot. Beth gazed in amazement at the array of clocks, dials, gauges and instruments that surrounded the two officers. When she looked out of the cockpit window, she saw that they were flying through thick cloud and she thought that the Captain must be very clever indeed to fly the plane without being able to see where they were going.

The clouds had cleared, and it was sunny but

cold when they arrived in Oslo. Beth was glad that she had packed her woollen jumper and winter coat. Unfortunately, they had only two hours before their next flight left for Senja, and there was no time to look at Oslo. Beth was sorry about this because, from the air, she had seen that Oslo was a beautiful city set at the top of a fjord, in which there were lots of little islands. She thought the islands looked just like a necklace of green jewels.

While they were waiting at the airport Beth had a fizzy lemonade, and something that her father called an open sandwich.

"But how can a sandwich be open?" she asked.

"Well, it is," Fred said. "See for yourself. It's a sort of sandwich without a lid on. I believe they eat a lot of them in these parts."

"It can't be a sandwich if it is open," said Beth stubbornly. "A sandwich is closed—meat, or cheese, or egg or something, shut up between two pieces of bread. This is a slice of bread with a bit of ham on top. It isn't a sandwich—not what I call a sandwich."

"Look, clever-socks," said Fred, with a sigh, "never mind what it is. Just eat it, eh?"

Beth did eat it, and found it so good that she ate two more. All the same, she held firmly to her opinion that a real sandwich had to have two slices of bread, not one.

They flew to Senja in a smaller aeroplane. The air was clean and bright, and below them they could see the tops of mountains covered in snow, looking like giant dollops of ice cream, and dozens of lakes and fjords, shining like strips of silver in the sunlight. There were forests, too, with hundreds of huge Christmas trees lining the mountain slopes as if they were sentries guarding the approach to Lapland.

Beth hardly said a word on the journey north. She was too thrilled by the view from the cabin window, too excited. She just sat there, with Battersea on her lap, staring out. Fred was so surprised by her silence that he said:

"Are you all right, Beth?"

Beth nodded her head.

"You are not feeling sick?"

Beth shook her head. Being sick was the last thought on her mind!

When they landed on the little airfield at Senja it was getting dark, and Beth felt as if she had just woken from a beautiful dream.

It was then that the hitch came.

They were met in the airport building by an

extremely tall, thin man who was dressed all in blue. He wore a blue suit, a blue shirt, a blue bow tie, blue gloves and blue suede shoes. Within all this blueness, his face stood out like a plate of cold porridge with two prunes in it for eyes.

Beth did not like the look of the Blue Man at all and she liked the sound of him even less, for when he spoke his voice was sharp and grating. It reminded her of the noise a spoon makes when you scrape out a saucepan and she felt a funny little tingle run across her teeth. When she heard the voice she knew in her bones that something was about to go wrong.

"I am Mr Roland Poley," the Blue Man said.

Beth only just managed to stop herself from laughing out loud. Roland Poley! Roley-poley! She had never seen anyone who looked less like a roley-poley. This man was as thin as a lollipop stick!

Mr Poley seemed to guess what Beth was thinking, for he glared at her with his dark eyes as if he were daring her to laugh. Fred saved the day by holding out his hand.

"Pleased to meet you, Mr Poley," he said.

After a moment of hesitation, Mr Poley shook Fred's outstretched hand, but he did so as if he were

touching a piece of cold wet fish and didn't much like it. Beth noticed that he did not remove his glove. She thought that this was rather rude. She had been told that when you shake hands you should always take off your glove.

Fred then introduced himself, and Beth and Battersea. Mr Poley looked at the dog and sniffed. It was a very long and disdainful sniff. Battersea gave a little murmuring growl and snuggled into Beth. Beth shivered and held Battersea a little closer. There was something about Mr Poley that made the air around him seem damp and cold and shivery.

"Have the letters and postcards for Father Christmas arrived?" asked Fred.

"They came by ship this morning," answered Mr Poley. He was still looking at Battersea in disapproval.

"Goodo," said Fred. "Then we should be able to leave in the helicopter tomorrow morning."

Mr Poley removed his cold dark eyes from the dog and fixed them on Fred.

"No," he said.

"No?" said Fred. "Why? Isn't the helicopter ready?"

"The helicopter is ready and the mailbags have

46

already been placed on board," said Mr Poley.

"Then everything is in order?" said Fred.

"In one sense, yes," said Mr Poley carefully. "But in another sense, no."

Fred scratched his head with one hand and stroked his chin with the other. He was obviously puzzled.

"Would you mind telling me what you are talking about?" he asked.

Mr Poley paused for a moment. He cleared his throat, making a noise like water gurgling down the plughole of a bath.

"The situation is," he said, at last, "the situation is this: you will not be going on the helicopter."

"Not going!" Fred looked astounded. "Not going! But who is going to deliver the letters and postcards?"

"I am," Mr Poley said.

"Ho," said Fred, and Beth could tell by his tone that her father was getting angry. "Ho. And who might you be, if it's not a rude question?"

Mr Poley lifted his head and straightened his back, so that he looked even taller. "I am from DOSSIE."

"I once knew a postman called Dossie," said Fred. "His real name was Charlie Magozelthorpe,

47

but we called him Dossie because he was always falling asleep.''

Mr Poley snorted irritably. "You must have heard of the organisation. You must have heard of DOSSIE."

"No," Fred said. "To tell you the truth, I haven't. I've heard of SWANK. I've seen that written on the back of hundreds of envelopes. It stands for Sealed With A Nice Kiss. I've heard of PAW, which means People Against War. I've even heard of DAFT—"

"DAFT?" interrupted Mr Poley.

"It was written up above the mirror in the toilet at the Post Office," said Fred. "DAFT. It means Don't Ask For Trouble. Oh, yes, I've heard of SWANK, PAW and DAFT, but I've never heard of DOSSIE. Have you, Beth?"

Beth shook her head. A little flush, the colour of raspberry-flavoured yoghurt, appeared in Mr Poley's cheeks.

"DOSSIE," he said, "DOSSIE stands for the Department Of Special Secrets, International Establishment."

"Fancy that," said Fred.

"And I am a Special Agent in the Father Christmas Section," continued Mr Poley. "It is our responsibility to protect the secret of Father Christmas. There are many people who would like to discover where he lives. It is my job to stop them getting this information."

"Well, I'm with you there," Fred said. "A hundred per cent on your side. Wouldn't do for everyone to know where he lives. It would spoil things."

"Exactly," said Mr Poley. "I am glad that you agree."

"But what exactly has all this to do with me?" asked Fred.

"Well, you must see that we can't possibly let you deliver the letters and cards," said Mr Poley. "If we did, both you and your daughter would learn the secret."

"Postman William always used to do the delivery," said Fred.

"Yes," said Mr Poley. "I am aware of that. And I did not like the arrangement."

Looking at Mr Poley's long, gloomy face, Beth had the feeling that there were a great many things he did not like. Leaving people alone was one of them.

"The fewer people who know the secret, the better it will be," Mr Poley continued. "And so the Father Christmas Section of DOSSIE has decided that all deliveries in future will be made only by one of our Special Agents."

"Meaning you?" said Fred.

"Precisely. Exactly. Absolutely," said Mr Poley.

"You want to make the delivery?" Fred spoke quietly, but there was a sharp edge to his voice.

"I do," said Mr Poley. "So I should be obliged if you would let me have your Letter of Authority." And he held out a thin, bony hand.

"Ho," Said Fred. "Ho. That's the game, is it? Well, you listen to me! I don't know about DOSSIE and I don't much care. What I *do* know is that those letters and cards are the responsibility of the Royal Mail. They are in our care until they are delivered.

And they can only be delivered by a Qualified Postman."

"Meaning you?" asked Mr Poley.

"Precisely. Exactly. Absolutely," said Fred.

"And the Letter of Authority?" Mr Poley's voice crackled like ice breaking on a pond, and it was twice as cold.

"Is staying in my pocket! Good day to you, sir," said Fred. "Come on, Beth."

And he led Beth away, leaving Mr Poley standing there, his porridgey face glowering out of the blueness that surrounded him.

"We shall see about this!" he shouted. "We shall see about this!"

But Fred did not bother to answer him.

5

That night Fred and Beth and Battersea stayed at a hotel called the Saga. They had a very nice room, and from the window they could see the lights of the boats bobbing about in the harbour and hear the water lapping against the shore. A crescent moon hung in the sky surrounded by thousands of twinkling stars.

After they'd both had a good wash and changed their clothes, Beth and Fred decided to go downstairs for some supper. But, just as they were about to leave, there was a knock at the door.

"Who is it?" called Fred.

"Here is Bo Swedberg," came the reply, in a low voice.

When Fred opened the door, they saw a young woman standing there. She was tall and blonde, and she had the bluest eyes that Beth had ever seen: they were as blue as a summer sky. She was wearing a dark red uniform, that had rings on the sleeves and bars on the shoulders made of gold braid.

"Are you perhaps Postman Fred?" the young woman asked in a whisper. She spoke with an odd accent, and she sometimes put words the wrong way round, but it was really rather pleasant.

"Yes, I am," replied Fred cautiously. Since their encounter with Mr Roland Poley he had decided to be careful with strangers.

"Ah. Good. Excellent. May I enter perhaps?" said the young woman.

Fred hesitated. He was still doubtful. But Battersea, who was an excellent judge of people, set his mind at rest. He jumped up at the young woman, his tail wagging in welcome. She smiled and patted his head. The smile was so warm and friendly that Fred could not help smiling back.

"Come in, please," he said.

She came in quickly and closed the door. "Ah, this is better," she said. "Allow me properly to introduce myself. I am Bo Swedberg. It is I who shall be taking you on your journey tomorrow."

"You?" said Fred, looking surprised.

"You are looking surprised. You do not think perhaps that a woman can fly a helicopter?"

"No—" said Fred, "I mean yes! Of course." He

looked embarrassed. "I don't see why women—I mean ladies, I mean yes—why not?"

"Good. Excellent," said Bo.

"I hope so," Fred said, "I sincerely hope so."

Bo turned to Beth. "And you are Beth, I think?"

"That's right," said Beth. "And this is Battersea."

"I am pleased to meet you all," said Bo. "I am sure we shall have a very happy journey."

"Do you know exactly where we are going?" asked Beth.

"Not yet," said Bo. "I shall not know until a few minutes before we take off, when I am given the Sealed Orders." She turned to Fred. "Now, excuse please. I must ask you. Have you the Letter of Authority?"

"Here," Fred said, patting his inside pocket. "Safe and sound."

"May I look at it?"

"I don't see why not," said Fred and took out the letter. Bo read it carefully, then handed it back with a nod.

"That is all in order, I think," she said. "But you must be very careful. There are people, bad people, who very much would like to get hold of that letter."

54

"I think we have already met one of them," said Fred. He told Bo all about their meeting with Mr Poley. As he did so, she frowned and shook her head.

"This man is bad," she said, "very bad."

"I didn't like the look of him," Fred said. "He was as cold as a cemetery in winter."

"He is a spy," continued Bo. "For years he has been trying to find the place where Father Christmas lives."

"He said he was from an organisation called DOSSIE," said Fred.

"That is a trick. There is no DOSSIE. It comes from his head—he makes it up."

"What would he do if he found out where Father Christmas lives?" asked Beth.

"It would be terrible!" answered Bo. "He would sell tickets to that place to hundreds of thousands of people all over the world. Father Christmas would have no peace to do his work. There would be hundreds of motorcars and coaches and buses, and there would be people everywhere—taking photographs, asking for autographs, making a disturbance. And from all this, Mr Poley would a fortune make: a million pounds or more perhaps. This is why you must keep the Letter of Authority safe."

"I will," Fred said. "Don't worry."

"I am sure," said Bo. "But you must careful be of Mr Poley. He is dangerous. He has many faces."

"What do you mean?" asked Fred.

"How do you say—he has disguises."

"Ah," said Fred. "I see. Well, we'll watch out for him, won't we, Beth?"

"We surely will!" agreed Beth. And Battersea barked.

"Good," said Bo. "Now, we shall depart in the morning at six o'clock. I hope this is not too early for you?"

"I'm a postman," said Fred. "Postmen are used to getting up early. We are on the streets when most people are still asleep."

"Of course," she said with a smile. "I will leave you now."

"Look, we were just going down to have some supper. Would you like to come too?" Fred said.

"Alas, I cannot," she said. "I have to prepare the helicopter. Thank you all the same. I will see you at six o'clock then."

"Six it is," said Fred. "Goodnight, Miss Swedberg."

"No, please," she said. "You must call me Bo, since we are friends."

"Okey-doke," said Fred. "Goodnight, Bo."

"Goodnight, Fred. And Beth. And also Battersea," she said.

"Well," said Fred, after he had closed the door. "A lady flying a helicopter! Wonders will never cease."

"I'd like to be a helicopter pilot when I am old enough," said Beth.

"Ho," said Fred. "I thought you were going to be a poet."

"Poets don't earn much money," said Beth. "So I shall be a helicopter pilot during the week, and write poems on Saturdays and Sundays!"

6

Soon after this, Fred and Beth went down to the hotel dining room for supper. Fred ordered a large steak, well-done, with chips for himself, and he was surprised when Beth ordered the same.

"A large steak might be a bit too much for you," said Fred.

"Oh, I shan't eat it all," Beth said.

"But you mustn't waste good food," said her father. This was something that he was quite strict about.

"I shan't waste it, I promise," said Beth. And when she had eaten half the steak, she cut the rest up into little pieces and asked the waiter to put them into a plastic bag. "It is for Battersea," she said, and, when the waiter looked puzzled, she explained: "Battersea is our dog."

The waiter smiled and took her plate away. He

came back a few minutes later with the steak in a
bag and winked at Beth: "For Battersea. I have put
a bone in the bag also."

He handed the bag to Beth and then he gave
Fred a letter.

Fred was surprised. And he was even more
surprised when he opened the envelope and read
what was inside.

"It's from the Hotel Manager," he said, and
showed the note to Beth. This is what she read:

> Please meet me in the wine cellar in the basement of
> the hotel in five minutes. I have important news
> about your mission.
>
> *M Natick*
> The Manager

"I wonder what he wants?" said Beth.

"I'll just have to go and find out," said Fred. He
gave Beth the key to their room. "You go and give
Battersea his supper. I'll come up as soon as I've
finished with the manager."

"Do you think you ought to go?" asked Beth.

"Why not?" said Fred.

"I don't know," said Beth. "I just have a feeling
about it."

"Don't you worry," Fred said sternly. "I can take care of myself." When her father spoke like that, Beth knew that there was no point in arguing with him.

"All right," she said, "but please be careful."

Fred found the wine cellar at the bottom of the backstairs. The door was ajar and it seemed to be dark inside. He knocked and, pushing the door open wider, he went inside. A voice spoke from the inky blackness.

"Ah. Good evening. Please close the door."

Fred closed the door and it became even darker than before. He could see nothing.

"Where are you?" he called.

"Over here," answered the voice.

And suddenly all the lights went on, so quickly and so brightly that Fred blinked. He looked around. He saw a lot of racks on either side of the cellar mostly stacked with bottles of wine, although there were other stores also. On one rack, there were what seemed to be sacks of flour and dozens of packets of cornflakes, as well as tins of food. Two large, mysterious-looking barrels with taps stood on a specially strong rack.

Fred moved forward slowly, then stopped. "Where are you?" he called again.

Suddenly he heard a grating sound behind him and someone laughed—a strange, weird, cackling laugh. He turned quickly and saw a man standing with his back to the door. He saw also that the door was now bolted.

The man had brown hair, a beard and a moustache, and he was wearing a brown suit and a dark red bow tie.

"I have bolted the door so that we shall not be disturbed," said the man, and came towards Fred.

All at once, Fred knew who he was. He had changed his appearance, but there was no mistaking

the cold, damp, shivery feeling in the air around him.

I've been a fool, Fred said to himself. It was a trick. I should never have come. I've been a silly fool! And, because he was angry with himself, he stepped forward, took hold of the man's beard and gave it a very sharp tug.

The man squealed and the beard came off with a sound like the tearing of cloth. There was no doubt about it now: he was Mr Poley.

"Ho," said Fred. "It's you again!"

Mr Poley rubbed his sore chin and glared at Fred. "I suppose you think you are very clever!" he said.

"No," Fred said, "I don't. I've been a fool. I should have guessed that note was from you! Now, if you don't mind, I am going!"

"Oh, no, you are not," said Mr Poley.

"Oh, yes, I am," said Fred.

"Not before you have given me your Letter of Authority!"

"You will never get that!" said Fred.

"We shall see!" said Mr Poley.

He made a sudden charge forward, but Fred was ready for him and he stepped to one side quickly. Mr Poley missed Fred and crashed into the rack, holding the sacks of flour. One of the sacks fell off, hitting Mr Poley and knocking him to the ground. At the same time the sack burst open and the flour spilled out over his head.

As Mr Poley lay there, coughing and spluttering and trying to wipe the flour from his eyes, Fred took hold of his arm and pulled him along the floor, until he lay under the mysterious-looking barrels.

Fred thought for a moment, scratching his head with one hand and stroking his chin with the other, and then he opened the taps on the barrels. To his surprise, honey and orange juice came lolloping out on to Mr Poley! They poured over him, mixing with the flour, and soon he was covered in sticky, reddy-brown dough.

Gasping and gurgling, Mr Poley tried to stand up but his feet slid in a puddle of honey and—zoomps!—down he went again. The more he struggled the worse it became.

Fred felt a lot better now. In fact, he felt quite chuffed. He unbolted the door and took one more look.

Mr Poley had given up the struggle, and he now lay still and quiet. His mouth was open and, every now and then, the honey dropped into it—plomp, plomp, plomp.

"I hope he has a sweet tooth," thought Fred as he went out.

He told Beth all about this little adventure and she scolded him for going to the cellar. But she wasn't really cross, for she had a picture in her mind of Mr Poley slithering about in that horrible mixture of honey, orange juice and flour. She made up a little poem about it:

A Problem for Mother Christmas

There was a stupid man who tried a stupid trick
Just because he was greedy for money.
But now he feels sore,
For he fell on the floor
All choked up with orange juice and honey!

7

It was still dark when they left the hotel the next morning but, by the time the taxi had reached the airport, the first streaks of morning light were touching the edge of the sky.

Bo was waiting for them and she led the way to the helicopter, which was guarded by two very stern-looking policemen.

"Just in case Mr Poley tries any more of his tricks," she said.

Fred and Beth, who was holding Battersea, climbed up the steps and took the two places behind Bo's seat. The mailbags with the letters and cards for Father Christmas were just behind them. Bo explained what Fred had to do.

"The mailbags are fastened already with the parachutes. There is also another bag here. It contains a Gorgonzola cheese and ten boxes of

liquorice allsorts. I am told that Father Christmas is very fond of Gorgonzola cheese and liquorice allsorts."

"He must be," said Fred.

"When we arrive at the house of Father Christmas," Bo continued, "I will give the signal. Then you must open the door at the back—here, like this."

And she opened a door at the back of the helicopter. "All you must then do," she continued, "is to push out the bags. The parachutes automatically will open and the bags will fall to the ground without hurt. You understand, I think?"

"I understand," said Fred. He was quite excited. It was the first time he had ever delivered letters by parachute.

"Have you done this trip before?" he asked Bo.

"No," she said. "This will be my first time. The pilot who used to take Postman William has retired also."

"Oh," said Fred.

"Do not worry, please," she said with a smile. "I have flown helicopters many times."

Just then, a big car drew up alongside the helicopter and a very important-looking man got out. He reminded Fred a little of Mr Smedley. He was carrying a letter which had a red seal as big as a fifty pence piece on the back of the envelope.

The man climbed the stairs of the helicopter and handed the letter to Bo, who was now sitting in the pilot's seat.

"Here are your Sealed Orders," he said. "You will not open the envelope until I have left and the door of the helicopter is closed."

"Thank you, Mr Andersen," said Bo.

The man turned to Fred. "Now," he said, "I must see your Letter of Authority."

Fred showed it to him and the man nodded. "You do understand that your mission is secret? Top Secret."

"Of course," said Fred.

"And you?" Mr Andersen looked at Beth. "When you get home you will not tell anyone where you have been and what you saw?"

"No," said Beth. "Cross my heart and hope to die." .

"Well, that's that," Mr Andersen said. And then he smiled, a kind smile, which made him look far nicer than Mr Smedley. "By the way," he continued, "I have some news of Mr Poley."

"Oh," said Fred.

"I don't think that he will trouble you again for a while. He is in hospital. Apparently the flour and the honey and the orange juice turned into a kind of hard pastry crust which stuck to his hair. If the doctors don't manage to remove it, he could go bald!"

"I've heard of mince pies," said Fred, "I've heard of steak and kidney pie, but this is the first time I've heard of a Mr Poley pie!"

Mr Andersen laughed. "Well," he said, "I wish you all good luck. I will see you back here this afternoon." Then, with a wave of his hand, he left them.

This afternoon, Beth thought. The man had said that he would see them this afternoon! She was surprised to think that the journey would be over so soon. And she was a little disappointed also, although she did not show it.

Bo closed the helicopter door and then turned her attention to the sealed envelope. She looked at Fred and Beth before she opened it. Beth felt her heart pounding as Bo broke the red seal. The Sealed Orders were now Unsealed!

Bo nodded her head as she studied the contents of the envelope. She took out a map and studied

70

that too, moving a finger across it.

"Everything all right?" asked Fred anxiously.

"I am thinking so. Yes. Everything is—how do you say—okey-doke?"

"Good," said Fred. "That's a relief."

"Please to fasten your seat belts," Bo said. "I must warn you—it will be noisy. It is best you wear your ear mufflers."

Fred and Beth fastened their belts and put on the mufflers. The engine of the helicopter had been running for some time but, as soon as the mufflers were over their ears, they could hardly hear it.

Bo gave them the thumbs-up sign and switched on the propeller. The great blades began to turn above them, slowly at first, but then with increasing speed. Beth slipped her mufflers aside for a moment and the sound of the propeller roared in her ears like a fierce wind in winter, only worse! She made a face and put the mufflers back quickly. Battersea, who was wearing the special coat Beth had made for him, buried his head in Beth's lap and put his paws over his ears.

8

A moment later, the helicopter began to rise from the ground. Soon it was circling high above the airport and the little town, and then it turned and flew over a short stretch of sea. The boats on the sea looked very small, not much bigger than the plastic boat Beth used to play with in the bath when she was smaller.

Before long, they were over land again, land that was mostly covered in snow. There were lots of big and not-so-big and small mountains, nestling together as if they were families. Sometimes the helicopter flew between the highest mountains, over valleys which were thick with trees, and sometimes Beth held her breath when a mountain loomed up in front of them, thinking for a moment that they were going to crash into it.

But she soon realised that there was no need to

worry, for Bo was a very good pilot and she seemed to know exactly what she was doing. Beth decided to relax and enjoy the flight.

After they had been flying for quite a long time, Bo began to look at the map more frequently. "We are getting near!" she shouted. Beth could not hear what she said because of the mufflers, but she guessed. And she again felt a tingling feeling of excitement, as if a whole army of pins and needles was jumping up and down and dancing in her stomach.

Then a strange thing happened. They came to a high range of snowy mountains, which were so close together that there was no space for the helicopter to get through. Bo flew along the range, which curved round and round so that it formed a complete circle, and in a few minutes they found themselves back where they started! Bo flew right round once more, a frown on her face.

She moved one of the controls, so that the helicopter stopped moving forward and simply hovered in midair with the propeller turning, then she signalled to Fred and Beth to take off their ear mufflers.

"This is the place," she shouted. "Just inside that ring of mountains."

"What's the trouble?" shouted Fred.

"I cannot fly over the mountains. They are too high. And I cannot see a space between the mountains where I can get through."

Ho, thought Fred. Now we have a problem. The words of the Post Office motto came into his mind:

Come sleet or rain, come hail or snow,
The letters and parcels have to go.

The motto did not say anything about mountains, but Fred knew that it was his duty to deliver the mail to Father Christmas. It simply had to be done!

"There must be a way," he shouted. "Postman William always delivered the letters and cards."

"I'll go round once more," she shouted.

The helicopter moved forward again. They all looked anxiously for a space wide enough to take the helicopter, but the mountains were like a

75

fortress. It was as if they were determined to keep out all intruders. Then suddenly Beth pointed downwards.

"There," she shouted, "there's a gap!"

And there was: a space between two mountains, about half-way up.

"I will take a look!" shouted Bo.

She allowed the helicopter to drop down until they were opposite the gap. It was very narrow, hardly wide enough to let the helicopter through.

"It will be a tight squeeze," shouted Bo.

"It is the only way!" shouted Fred.

76

Bo nodded. "I am thinking we might just manage it. Hold tight!"

She approached the gap very cautiously, and the helicopter flew forward between the two mountains. The space was wider than it had looked, but

even so, it seemed at moments that they were so close they could have reached out and touched the side of the mountain. And the rushing blades of the helicopter, sending out a current of air, disturbed the snow so that it slipped and poured down the mountainside like a great white river.

It seemed to be ages before they finished flying through the gap. And then came the greatest surprise of all, far bigger than any that had gone before!

A Problem for Mother Christmas

Suddenly, the ice, the snow and the fir trees were gone, and they found themselves flying over a sunny green valley! Down below there were meadows, little woods, a sparkling river and bushes bright with blossom. It was like a valley in England in springtime, only much more beautiful. It's tremendous, thought Beth, it's fabulous, it's magic. Yes, that was the word. It had to be magic, for how else could such a valley exist in Lapland, in that wilderness of snow and ice?

There were animals, too, all sorts of animals. Beth saw sheep and cows and goats grazing on the lush grass, and two horses trotting around in circles.

And, as if this wasn't enough, a flock of twelve huge birds came flying towards them. They were enormous, the most gigantic birds that Beth had ever seen!

As the birds drew near the helicopter, they separated into two groups and flew alongside, six on one side and six on the other, taking care not to get too near the propeller blades. It looked as if they had come to welcome the helicopter, and had formed themselves into an escort.

Then Beth realised that they were not birds at all. They were reindeer—flying reindeer!

9

After a few minutes, the two groups of reindeer wheeled away from the helicopter and joined up together, making a shape in the sky like a pointed kite or an arrow. The reindeer at the tip of the formation dipped towards the ground, as if to salute the helicopter, and then led the way downwards. Considering how big they were, Beth

thought they were very graceful, just as graceful as a flight of swallows.

Then she pointed excitedly to the ground. The reindeer were landing one by one in a green field, and next to the field there was a house: a sort of farmhouse with a roof of red tiles and a little white streamer of smoke curling out of the chimney.

"That's it!" shouted Beth. "That must be it. Father Christmas's house!"

Bo nodded. "Get ready!" she shouted, and she made the helicopter go lower until it hovered about 200 metres in the air above the front of the house.

Fred went to the back of the helicopter to get ready to drop the mailbags while Beth peered out of the window anxiously. Oh, how she wished that they could land and actually see Father Christmas and speak to him! Perhaps, at the very least, he would come out of the house and wave to them. But, alas, the reindeer were grazing in the field, some chickens were pecking about at the front of the house, but she could see not one human being.

Yet Father Christmas must be at home or nearby. Otherwise, why should there be smoke from the chimney?

For a moment, she thought she saw a glimpse of a face peering at them from an upstairs window, but when she looked again it was gone. I must have imagined it, she thought.

Then she noticed something rather odd on the little strip of lawn in front of the house. Someone had arranged dozens and dozens of what seemed to be dolls in a pattern on the grass. Beth was not properly sure that they *were* dolls, so she borrowed Bo's binoculars and had a closer look.

Yes, they were dolls all right; dolls of all sorts, sizes and colours. And then she noticed something else. The dolls had been set out in such a way as to form three huge letters. She made out an S then an O and then another S: S O S.

Beth knew what the letters meant because she had read a library book about the adventures of an English family who went round the world in a

yacht: when the yacht hit a reef in the South Seas, they had to send out a special call for help on their radio. It was called a Distress Signal and had to be sent in code, Morse Code, tapping out the letters S–O–S. Anyone hearing those letters would know at once that help was needed.

But did it mean that Father Christmas was in distress, that he needed help?

"I'm all ready!" Fred shouted from the back of the helicopter.

"Wait!" replied Beth, and pointed to the letters on the lawn below them.

Both Fred and Bo looked down. Then they looked at each other, and looked down again. Fred scratched his head with one hand and stroked his chin with the other.

"S O S," said Bo. "It means that help is necessary."

"Do you think we should land and take a look?" asked Fred.

"Oh, no!" replied Bo. "It is extremely forbidden to land."

"But we must!" cried Beth. "Father Christmas might be ill!"

"It is against orders," said Bo, shaking her head.

82

"Can't you speak on the radio to—whatshis-name—Mr Andersen, and ask him what to do?" asked Fred.

Bo shook her head again. "Is not possible. These high mountains all around this place—they stop the radio signal. I cannot get through to Mr Andersen, or anyone else."

"We can't just drop the bags and leave!" Beth said. "Listen, Bo. No one will know if we do land for a few minutes."

"I will know," Bo said. "The Sealed Orders say not to land. I cannot go against the Orders. I am so sorry."

They all looked at each other. Then Fred said suddenly: "I know! I have it!"

"Pardon?" said Bo.

"Look," Fred said. "SOS is the International Distress Signal. Right?"

"That is correct," said Bo.

"And a Distress Signal comes before anything else. Right?"

"I do not understand," said Bo.

"Well," said Fred, "suppose you were captain of a ship with orders to sail, say, from London to New York. Halfway across the Atlantic you hear an SOS on your radio, a Distress Signal which told you that a ship was sinking two hundred miles away. What would you do?"

"I should, of course, go to help the ship," said Bo.

"You would forget your orders and go to the rescue?"

"Naturally—yes."

"Good!" said Fred. "This isn't a ship, it is a helicopter. But the same rule applies. When you receive a Distress Signal you forget about orders, Sealed or otherwise, and go to the rescue."

Brilliant, Beth thought, brilliant! If she had not been strapped in her seat she would have hugged her father.

But Bo was not so sure. A little furrow appeared on her forehead as she thought about the problem. Then, at last, she smiled.

"Very well. We shall go down. But we will not stay long."

And she took the helicopter down, down, down, very slowly and carefully, until it landed on the ground with a little shudder. The chickens fled for their lives, clucking and cackling, as the wind from the great blades of the propeller stirred the grass and bent the branches of the trees. Then gradually the propeller stopped and all was still.

10

They soon had yet another surprise. The front door of the house opened as they got out of the helicopter and someone came out. Beth had expected to see Father Christmas but it was not him at all—it was a woman!

Beth had always believed that Father Christmas lived alone and she was quite surprised, although she was too polite to show it.

"Hello!" said the surprise woman briskly. "That's a very rackety, clackety machine you have there. The noise frightened my chickens out of their feathers. I doubt if they will lay any eggs for a week!"

She was quite a plump, jolly person with pink cheeks and smiling brown eyes. Her hair was hidden under a white cloth and she wore blue dungarees with straps which fastened over her

85

shoulders. On her feet she had a pair of green wellington boots, and she carried a big rake.

She held out a hand: "Pleased to meet you."

"Likewise," said Fred. He introduced Beth and Bo and Battersea. The woman shook their hands up and down several times with a very firm grip.

"Ah," she said to Bo. "You fly that machine, do you?"

"That is so," said Bo politely.

"Good!" said the woman. "And I bet that you do it just as well as a man, eh?" She chuckled at this, a long cheerful chuckle that seemed to start in her stomach and work its way up until it came out of her mouth, and she slapped Bo on the back so hard that she staggered a little.

Bo could not think of anything to say, so she coughed and replied: "Thank you. I am thanking you very much."

"Don't mention it," said the woman.

"Excuse me," said Fred.

"Yes?"

"I don't want to be rude," said Fred, "but would you mind telling me to whom I have the pleasure of speaking?"

"Pardon?" said the woman. She looked puzzled.

"What I mean is— who are you?" asked Fred bluntly.

Now the woman looked rather disgusted. "You mean— you don't know?"

"I haven't a clue," said Fred. "Sorry."

"Isn't that always the way," she said, and made a tut-tutting sound with her gums. "You know *him*, of course. Everybody writes letters to *him*! The whole world knows who *he* is."

"Knows who?" asked Fred.

"Why, Father Christmas! You know who he is. But you have never heard of me."

"Sorry," said Fred. He was a little embarrassed and shuffled his feet.

"No need to be sorry," said the woman, more

cheerfully. "It's not your fault. If you must know, I am Mrs Christmas."

"Mrs Christmas!" Beth could not hide her surprise now. As far as she knew, nobody had ever heard of a Mrs Christmas.

"That's right," said the woman, with a smile. "But you can call me Mother Christmas."

"Ho!" Fred said. "This is a discovery. I wonder what they'll say back there when we tell them!"

"I hope they'll be pleased," said Mother Christmas, more cheerfully, and she went on, "you must excuse these clothes but I was just mucking out the reindeer stables. Very mucky animals reindeers, you know. Muckier than two monkeys in a barrel of mud. But I mustn't keep you standing out here. Come inside."

She turned to lead the way into the house, but Beth stopped her: "Mother Christmas!"

"Yes?"

"Please—could you explain? The valley is so green and bright—but outside, beyond the mountains, there is only ice and snow."

"Very simple," said Mother Christmas. "Those high mountains keep out the snow and cold winds. And we have hot springs and underground streams that keep the earth warm. Very simple."

Beth did not think it was as simple as all that, more like magic. But she didn't ask any more questions. Bo was the next to speak.

"Excuse please, but what is the meaning of these?" asked Bo, and she pointed to the dolls set out on the lawn.

"The meaning?" said Mother Christmas. "Can't you read? It stands out like the nose on my pet pig! S–O–S."

"This I know," said Bo patiently. "I am asking—does it mean that you are in need of help?"

"Are you in trouble?" asked Fred. "That's what we want to know."

"Oh, no," said Mother Christmas. "I am not in trouble. Definitely not!"

"Then we cannot stay," Bo said. "If you have no trouble, we must at once leave."

"I said *I* am not in trouble," said Mother Christmas. "But someone is—oh, yes, someone is in a great deal of trouble!"

"Who?" asked Fred.

"Why, you, of course," said Mother Christmas. "All of you. Up to your eyebrows in trouble."

Fred scratched his head with one hand and stroked his chin with the other. "Would you mind saying that again, please?"

"Certainly," said Mother Christmas. "I said that you are up to your eyebrows in trouble."

"How is that?" asked Fred.

"Because," said Mother Christmas slowly, "because unless you can do something—and do it quickly—there will be no Father Christmas calling on the children next Christmas. No Father Christmas, no sledge, no reindeer and no presents. Nothing!"

"No Father Christmas!" said Bo.

"No Father Christmas!" said Fred.

"No Father Christmas!" cried Beth.

And they all looked at each other. It was impossible to think of Christmas without Father Christmas. It just would not be the same. It would be a tragedy, a calamity!

"No Father Christmas," said Mother Christmas firmly. "Now, come inside and I will tell you all about it."

As she led the way in, she called, "Tom! Tom! Visitors!"

11

Tom?

Beth wondered who on earth this could be, but she did not have to wonder for long. She heard someone call "Yippee!" and, looking up, she saw a boy at the top of the stairs.

But, in the very next second, he lay at Beth's feet looking up at her, for he had slid down the stair rail, dropped on to the polished floor of the hall and slithered towards her.

"Hi, girl!" he said, with a cheeky smile.

"Hi, boy," replied Beth coldly. She didn't like being called 'girl'.

"Tom, Tom!" said Mother Christmas. "How many times have I told you not to slide down that stair rail! You'll do yourself an injury one day!" She turned to the others: "This rascal is my son, Tom."

Tom picked himself up and grinned. He was

about the same age as Beth, but not quite so tall.

Fred and Bo said hello to Tom, and Battersea barked.

"Is that your dog?" Tom asked Beth.

"Yes," replied Beth. "His name is Battersea. Do you like dogs?"

"No," said Tom.

"Oh," said Beth. She was quite disappointed.

"Don't fret, my dearie," said Mother Christmas. "He means yes, don't you, Tom?"

"No," said Tom again. Beth was quite bewildered by now for although he said 'no', he nodded his head vigorously.

"Tom has a problem with his nos and his yesses, you see," said Mother Christmas. "He gets them mixed up. He says 'yes' when he means 'no', and 'no' when he means 'yes'."

"That must be very complicated," said Fred.

"Oh, no," Mother Christmas said happily, "you will soon get used to it."

Beth was not too sure about this but she didn't say anything.

"Now, Tom," continued Mother Christmas, "you take Beth and Battersea and show them the Grotto, while I have a chat with her father and Bo."

"Come on, girl," said Tom.

"Don't call me girl," said Beth, feeling a little bit cross. "My name is Beth."

"That's right, Beth," said Mother Christmas, "you tell the cheeky rascal where he gets off!"

Tom grinned and winked at Beth. She decided that she really could not be cross with him anymore. He seemed to be such a cheerful boy.

The adults went into the sitting room, and Tom led Beth and Battersea towards the back of the house and into a large kitchen. Beth felt quite warm in her winter coat so she took it off, and then she removed Battersea's jacket, too. He seemed relieved to be free of it and sat down at once to have a good scratch.

"Are you thirsty?" Tom asked.

"Yes, I am quite," she said.

"Would you like a glass of sour reindeer milk?" said Tom.

Beth considered this. Reindeer milk might have been acceptable but *sour* reindeer milk didn't sound very nice. So she said in her best polite voice, "No, I don't think so, thank you very much."

"A cup of hot custard?" asked Tom.

"No, thank you," said Beth. She quite liked custard with plum pudding or mince pie but she did not like the idea of drinking it. And still trying to be polite, she continued: "Would you have some water, by any chance?"

"No," said Tom.

Beth thought it strange that there should be no water in the house, but then she remembered what Mother Christmas had said. Of course! When Tom said 'yes', he meant 'no'. She decided to test him.

"In that case, I think I will have a glass of water," she said.

And it worked! Tom said: "Very well. I'll get you some."

Beth watched him as he filled a beaker from a large glass container and gave it to her. She sipped it cautiously. It was delicious, the finest water she had ever tasted!

94

"It's great!" she said.

"It's just dew," he said. "Don't you drink dew at home?"

"No," Beth said. "I'm afraid we don't!"

"You must live in a very strange place if you don't drink dew," he said scornfully.

"Where does it come from?" she asked.

"Where does it come from?" he said even more scornfully. "Where does it come from? It is there every morning, on the grass and the flowers and the bushes!"

Beth wanted to ask him how they collected the dew but she decided that this would only give him a chance to be scornful again, so she held her tongue. She drank the beaker of dew slowly, letting it trickle down her throat, and it seemed to cool and freshen her whole body. Then she poured some of the dew into a bowl for Battersea and he lapped it up eagerly.

Tom took a tin from a cupboard and opened it. "Would you like a sausage roll?" he asked.

"I wouldn't mind. Thank you," said Beth.

She took a sausage roll from the tin and bit into the brown flaky pastry on the outside. But when she got to the inside, she had yet another surprise. Instead of sausage—what she called sausage—she found a mixture of nuts and apple, with just a hint of peppermint.

"Don't you like it?" he asked, watching her face.

"Oh, yes," she said, which was the truth, for it was just as delicious as the dew. She threw a piece to Battersea, who caught it in his mouth and swallowed it almost in one movement. He must have liked it too, for he stood wagging his tail for more.

"Don't you have sausage rolls where you come from?" asked Tom.

"Oh, yes," she answered. "But they are not the same."

"If they are not the same," he said, "then they can't be sausage rolls, can they?"

"I wouldn't call this a *sausage* roll," said Beth. "Not a proper sausage roll. It is very nice. But I would call it a fruit and nut roll—with peppermint."

"You *do* come from a peculiar country," Tom said. And once again, Beth decided that it would be better not to argue. He was a very cheerful boy but he was quite infuriating also!

"Come," said Tom, "I'll show you the Grotto."

He opened a small green door at one side of the

kitchen. It was so small that Beth banged her head as she went through.

"Whoops!" Tom said. "Mind your head!"

"It is a bit late to say that!" Beth said crossly, rubbing her forehead.

It was pitch black inside the Grotto and all Beth could see was an odd twinkle and glitter in the far darkness. Battersea began to bark and the sound seemed to bounce back from the walls like a great echo. Beth picked him up and hushed him into silence.

And then, Tom pulled a big switch and a thousand lights came on, lights so bright that Beth blinked her eyes. But it wasn't just the lights that made her blink, it was what she saw.

Before her was a huge cavern, an enormous cavern, higher than Big Ben, wider than ten or even twelve tennis courts, and longer than a whole street of houses! She could hardly believe her eyes. From the helicopter she had seen only a small farmhouse and some barns—not a sign of this fantastic place! It was as if she had opened a cupboard door at home and found that the inside was as big as the Albert Hall! It was magic, yet another piece of magic!

The Grotto had a rocky roof and rocky walls and,

except for the little corridors between, it was stacked from floor to ceiling with toys and similar things: large toys, small toys, medium toys; train sets, cars, puzzles, dolls, teddy bears, pandas, perambulators, cots, coloured balls, games, Action Men, bicycles, tricycles, building bricks, Lego, fireworks, toy typewriters, musical instruments and books—thousands and thousands of different books—and thousands and thousands of other things.

There were tee shirts and sports shirts and tracksuits; tennis racquets, cricket bats, hockey sticks and table tennis sets; model-making sets, pocket calculators, video games, painting sets, woodwork sets, needlework sets and every other kind of set you could think of!

And the bright lights, glinting on all these things, reflected a whole rainbow of colours on the roof and walls.

It was amazing, stunning, terrific, brilliant! And it was a whole minute, sixty seconds, before Beth found the breath to speak.

"These are the presents!" she whispered, at last. "These are the presents that Father Christmas delivers on Christmas Eve!"

"No," said Tom.

But Beth noticed just in time that he was nodding his head and realised that he meant yes.

"But they won't be delivered this year," Tom continued sadly.

"Why ever not?" asked Beth.

"Well, for one thing, they are not wrapped up, are they?" said Tom.

Heavens, thought Beth, it would be impossible to wrap all these presents. It would take ages and ages!

"That's only part of the problem," Tom continued. "You see, we can't find my father." There was a little tremble in his voice, as if he were near to tears.

"You can't find Father Christmas!" exclaimed Beth. She could hardly believe her ears. Then she added gently, because she felt sorry for him, "Tell me what happened, Tom."

"I don't know," Tom said. "All I know is that he is lost and we can't find him."

12

In the parlour, Mother Christmas was explaining all this to Fred and Bo.

"But you cannot lose Father Christmas!" said Bo.

"It does seem rather careless," said Fred.

"It is all very well for you to sit there like a parrot on a perch and talk," said Mother Christmas crossly, "but that is exactly what *has* happened. He is lost." And then, with a sigh, she added: "I suppose it is my fault really."

"How can that be?" asked Bo.

"Well," said Mother Christmas, "we had a slight difference of opinion." She sighed. "The trouble is that when he comes back home after each Christmas, he goes straight to bed."

"I can understand that!" said Fred. "He must be blooming tired. I am a Qualified Postman and I know that delivering is very hard work. And he has to go down all those chimneys with all those parcels! Phew—it makes me break into a sweat just thinking of it!"

And he mopped his forehead with the clean handkerchief he kept in his top pocket.

"Oh, I knew he was tired," said Mother Christmas. "I could understand if he slept for a week. But it was more than that. This year, when he came back, he stayed in bed for over a month."

"A month!" said Fred.

"Four weeks and three days," said Mother Christmas solemnly, "without a word of a lie. He stayed in that bed from Christmas Day until the third of February."

"Hmph," said Fred, "that is rather a long time. What you might call an excessively long time."

"To sleep for a month!" Bo said. "He must have been very tired."

"Oh, he didn't sleep that long," said Mother Christmas. "He woke up on Boxing Day. He said he wanted to rest a bit more and that he'd decided to stay in bed. So I took him up his breakfast, his lunch and his supper. The next day it was the same. And the next. And the next week. And the next.

And the next. The only time he got up was to go to the bathroom."

"Was he ill?" asked Fred.

"No, no," said Mother Christmas. "He was as chirpy as a garden full of birds. As bright as a basket of oranges. Mind you, that's no change. He's always cheerful—and he gets up to more mischief than a wagonload of monkeys. The only time he's grumpy is when he is hungry. He likes his food."

"But he would not get up?"

"No."

"Very worrying for you," Fred said.

"You can say that again," said Mother Christmas.

"Very worrying for you," said Fred, happy to oblige.

"And it was tiring, too," she said. "Up and down, up and down, up and down the stairs a dozen times a day, with trays of food and drinks and suchlike. But what worried me most was next Christmas."

"I can see that," Fred said.

"I mean, it takes us a whole year to get the presents wrapped and ready. And we always have a terrible rush in November and December, what with all the letters that come in and the labelling that has to be done. It is near the end of February now and we haven't even started. I've been too busy running about after him and looking after the animals. We shall never catch up at this rate!"

"Didn't you tell Father Christmas all this?" asked Fred.

"Tell him? I told him until I was blue in the face! If I told him once, I told him a hundred times. But all he said was not to worry, everything would be all right. I tell you, he wore me out!"

She sat down with a 'plomp' in an armchair and Fred could see that she looked very tired.

"Well," continued Mother Christmas, "last week I decided that it could not go on any longer.

I'd got to the end of my tether. I told him that there was work to be done, and that he had better get up and help."

"What did he say to that?" asked Fred.

"He turned all grumpy, didn't he! Very grumpy and growly, like a bear with a sore head. Not like him at all. I said he could be as grumpy as he liked, but I was not going to wait on him any longer. No more trays—no breakfast in bed, no lunch, no supper. He went even more grumpy then, very grumpy indeed. All next day he just stayed in bed, thumping on the floor with his stick and calling for his dinner."

"You did not take him the dinner?" asked Bo.

"No. And that man can't bear to go without his

dinner. Do you know, I've seen him eat six fried eggs with eight fried bananas and a heap of turnips, cabbage, spinach and potatoes, followed by nut and raspberry crumble with custard and reindeer cream, and then hold out his plate for more. Where food is concerned his mouth is an ever-open door."

She paused for breath. "Well," she went on, "the longer he laid in bed, the hungrier he became. He grew hungrier and hungrier, and grumpier and grumpier. And the next morning he wasn't in his bed any more."

"He got up?" asked Fred.

"Not only did he get up—he vanished. At first, I thought he was just teasing us, playing a joke. But now, I admit, I'm really worried." Fred saw tears glistening in her eyes.

"Where could he have gone?" Bo asked.

"Well, he is somewhere in the valley," said Mother Christmas, wiping her eyes with the corner of her apron. "He won't have crossed the mountains."

"Then it should be easy to find him," said Fred.

"Don't you believe it!" she answered. "Tom and I have hunted everywhere. This valley is full of hiding places. Caves and potholes and suchlike. And Father Christmas knows them all."

Fred scratched his head with one hand and stroked his chin with the other. "Well," he said, "well. This is a serious business. Very serious indeed. It has all the makings of a crisis."

"He must be found," said Bo. "Christmas will not be Christmas without him."

"And you really have no idea where he might be?" Fred asked Mother Christmas.

"That's a soppy question!" said Mother Christmas. "If I knew where he was he wouldn't be lost, would he? And I wouldn't be sitting here talking to you, would I?"

"No," Fred said, "I suppose not."

"No suppose about it," said Mother Christmas.

Fred got to his feet, looking very determined. "Bo," he said, "we have to search this valley until we find Father Christmas. This is an emergency. You take the helicopter, fly as close to the ground as you can, and look for him. Beth and I will go with Battersea on foot. We'll take young Tom along as a guide." He turned to Mother Christmas. "Have you any fireworks?"

"Thousands of them," she answered.

"Good," said Fred. "If I find him, Bo, I will set off a rocket to let you know. If you see where he is, circle over the place until we get there. Agreed?"

107

"Agreed!" said Bo.

"I'll make you a picnic in case you get hungry," said Mother Christmas.

"Right!" said Fred. "And then we'll begin the search right away!"

13

It was, indeed, a very strange valley. There were pleasant green meadows coloured with buttercups, dandelions and daisies, and gentle streams gurgling over the stones.

But every now and then, during the search, they came across great heaps of rocks all tumbled

together, huge rocks, many of them as big as a house. And in between the rocks there were all sorts of caves, some small and some big enough to live in.

Then there were places where hot springs belched out of the ground, forming pools of steamy water and sending off a peculiar smell. It made Beth think of rotting vegetables and of the smell of her father's compost heap in the garden at home, but Fred explained that it was the smell of sulphur.

There was even a jungle in one part of the valley, a small jungle to be sure, but it was a jungle all right: the tall trees and the bushes below them grew so close together, it was almost impossible to find a way through.

Beth was quite afraid of the jungle at first, thinking that it would be full of lions and tigers and spiders and snakes. She especially did not like snakes and told Tom so.

He laughed. "*I* like snakes," he said.

You would, thought Beth.

"All the animals and the snakes are my friends," he continued. "They know I will not harm them and I know they will not hurt me. Look—I tell you what. I will find you a snake and you can keep it as a pet."

110

"No, thank you very much!" said Beth quickly.

"A spider, then?"

"No, thank you!" said Beth firmly. "I have Battersea and he is all I want." She was half sure that Tom was teasing her, for she saw him wink at Fred.

Battersea barked when he heard his name mentioned, and then his attention was distracted by a large butterfly with purple, gold and white wings and he began to chase after it. But the butterfly skimmed along just in front of his nose quite happily, as if it were enjoying the game.

Well, they searched and searched. They poked around the caves, they looked in the long grass and among the trees, but there was no sign of Father

Christmas. Fred and Tom even forced their way through the jungle but they could not find him.

They kept a lookout for Bo in the helicopter but each time she flew over she shook her head. At last Fred called a halt. "He must be somewhere," he said. "But where is somewhere, that's the question. Let us stop here and think what to do."

They sat down in a meadow by the side of a stream and started on the picnic that Mother Christmas had prepared for them. There were cheese and apple sandwiches, tomato sandwiches, cucumber sandwiches, banana fritters, fruit buns and bottles of that delicious dew. Beth was quite pleased to see that they were proper sandwiches made with a nice slice of home-made bread on the top and bottom. She poured some dew into a dish for Battersea and gave him one of the special bone-shaped biscuits that she had brought with her from London.

They saw Bo flying overhead and waved for her to land. The helicopter made a great racket as it touched the ground, and flights of brightly-coloured birds, finches, budgerigars and parrots flew away from it in fright, screeching loudly. As soon as the propeller stopped Bo got out and joined the others.

"Did you see him?" asked Fred.

"No, I'm afraid not," answered Bo, helping herself to a cheese and apple sandwich.

"We have looked everywhere," said Fred. "Tom—have you any ideas?"

"He could be up a tree," said Tom.

"Up a tree!" said Beth. She thought that sounded very odd.

"He likes climbing to the top of a tall tree," said Tom.

"What does he do when he gets up there?" asked Fred.

"He just sits there. For hours and hours. He likes to look at the sky. He especially likes to watch the sky at night and study the stars."

"What goes up must come down," said Fred. "He can't sit up a tree forever. For one thing, he would get hungry. So he is sure to come back to earth sooner or later."

"Sometimes he stands on his head," said Tom calmly, helping himself to a cucumber sandwich.

"He does *what?*" exclaimed Fred in an amazed voice.

"Stands on his head," said Tom, munching away. "He says it helps him to see things the right way up."

113

"The right way up!" said Beth. "If you are standing on your head, I should think you would see things the wrong way up!"

"That depends on your point of view," said Tom.

"We are talking about the point of view!" argued Beth. "And if you stand on your head, you must have a topsy-turvy point of view."

Fred interrupted before Tom could answer.

"All right, all right. That's enough of that! What I want to know is—*where* does he stand on his head?"

"Anywhere," said Tom. "In the bedroom, in the kitchen, in the garden. On the roof sometimes."

"That doesn't help us much, does it!" said Fred, who sounded as if he was running out of patience. "It doesn't help us to *find* him!"

"He likes fishing," said Tom.

"And I suppose when he is fishing he stands on his head!" said Fred sarcastically.

"If the fancy takes him," said Tom.

"Where does he go fishing?" asked Beth.

"Usually he climbs to the top of one of the piles of rocks and fishes from there," he answered.

"But there is no water there!" said Beth. "No river, no fish!"

114

"He catches imaginary fish." Tom took yet another sandwich.

"Imaginary fish!" exclaimed Beth.

"He doesn't believe in catching real fish," said Tom. "He says that fish have feelings like anybody else, and how would human beings like it if they had a hook stuck in their mouths."

"I have read that fish do not have feelings," said Bo.

"You wouldn't say that if you were a fish," Tom said.

"No. You are right perhaps," said Beth thoughtfully.

"Father is a terrific fisherman," said Tom. "Last year he caught an imaginary salmon that weighed ten kilos."

"Ten kilos?" said Fred, who wasn't very good with kilograms and metres and suchlike.

"That's over twenty pounds," said Beth.

"That's big," said Fred, "very big indeed. A monster of a salmon!"

"What I don't understand," said Beth, "what I don't understand is this: if it was an *imaginary* salmon, how could he weigh it?"

"He uses imaginary scales, of course," replied Tom. He said it as if imaginary fish and imaginary scales were the most ordinary things in the world.

"He might just as well have said that the salmon weighed forty kilos," Beth said. "Even fifty or a hundred. If the fish was invisible, nobody would know."

"That would be cheating!" said Tom.

14

At that moment Battersea began to bark and, turning round, Beth saw a reindeer flying towards him with Mother Christmas on its back.

"Yippee!" called Mother Christmas, and she let

go of the reindeer's horns, waved both arms in the air, and shouted: "Look! No hands! I'm not holding on!"

The reindeer came gliding in to land, graceful as a swallow, and Mother Christmas slid down from his back.

"I thought you were supposed to be out searching," she said. "Not sitting down, feeding your faces!"

"We have been searching!" said Fred indignantly.

"We have miles walked and everywhere looked!" said Bo.

"All right," said Mother Christmas, "keep your hair on. I was only teasing. Listen, I've got news for you!"

"You have found Father Christmas!" cried Beth.

"No such luck," said Mother Christmas. "But something peculiar has happened. You remember that you brought some Gorgonzola cheese and boxes of liquorice allsorts as a present for him?"

"Of course," Fred said.

"You didn't bring them with you?"

"No," said Fred. "The last time I saw the bag, it was in the kitchen."

"That's right," said Mother Christmas. "Well,

after you'd gone, I went out to feed the chickens. And when I came back, the cheese and the allsorts were gone. And half of a batch of my sausage rolls."

"You mean, they've been stolen?" asked Fred.

"In a manner of speaking, yes," she replied, "and in a manner of speaking, no. I reckon he has taken them. And since they rightly belong to him, you can't really say they were stolen, can you?"

"That is logistic," said Bo.

"I think you mean logical," said Fred politely.

"Logical—yes," Bo said.

"If Father Christmas came to the house and took the cheese and the allsorts, then it means that he *is* in the valley," said Beth.

"And it means that he is hungry," said Bo.

"And it means that he can't be very far away," said Fred. He got to his feet. "Come on, everybody! We'll go back to the house to see if we can find any clues. Then we will start the search again. And this time we will look twice as carefully as before!"

"Have you ever ridden on a reindeer, Beth?" asked Mother Christmas.

"Never," said Beth.

"You do come from a peculiar place," Tom said. "I thought everyone rode on reindeers!"

"You be quiet, Tom," said Mother Christmas.

"One day, you'll trip over that tongue of yours. Come on, Beth. I'll give you a lift back."

She put two fingers to her mouth and made a shrill whistle. The reindeer came trotting over to her and Mother Christmas lifted Beth on to his back.

"Hold on tight to his horns, dearie," she said.

Tom vaulted on next, then Mother Christmas mounted and sat behind them both. Battersea lay crouched between Beth's knees. He looked up at her with very mournful eyes, as if he was wondering what on earth they would get up to next.

"Giddyup, Buster!" shouted Mother Christmas.

Buster, the reindeer, ran forward for a few strides and then launched himself into the air. At first, Beth was just a little bit afraid. She held on tight to the horns, her hair streaming in the wind and her eyes half closed, while Battersea hid his head in his paws. But the ride was so comfortable and Buster flew so gracefully that they soon began to enjoy themselves.

She had been thrilled by the ride in the helicopter, but this was even better and certainly much less noisy. Beth imagined that it must be rather like flying in a glider as they swooped and soared silently over meadows, hills, trees and rocks.

120

"Do you like it?" asked Mother Christmas.

"Fabulous!" replied Beth. "Really fabulous."

And she felt quite sorry when Buster set them down in the field next to the house. She patted his neck and thanked him, and he turned his head and gently muzzled her hand.

When they entered the kitchen, Mother Christmas suddenly exclaimed: "He has been here again!"

"How do you know?" asked Beth.

"I left six loaves of my home-made bread on the

table! Look, there are only four now. He has taken two!"

"Are you sure?"

"As sure as I am that apples have pips, doors have handles and water is wet! Oh, I don't mind him having the bread—I don't want him to go hungry. But he's a soppy old twerp, putting us to all this trouble!" She didn't sound cross, only sad.

Beth did not say anything, but in her heart she did not believe that Father Christmas was a twerp. She liked to think that sometimes he climbed trees to look at the stars, or stood on his head; that sometimes he caught imaginary fish and did all sorts of funny things.

She longed to see him. She could not possibly go home to England without meeting him. And she certainly could not go home and tell everyone that Father Christmas would not be calling on the children this year.

And, all of a sudden, she had one of her feelings. Something good was going to happen. Lots of exciting things had happened to her since she left England but this, she felt sure, would be the most exciting of all.

"Come on, Battersea," she said with fresh

determination, "we won't wait for the others. We'll start looking again."

"You might get lost," Tom said.

"I don't think so," Beth replied.

"All the same, I think I'd better come along," he said.

"I don't want you to come because you think I need someone to look after me," she said. "You can come only if you really want to. Do you want to?"

"No," he said.

Beth was used to Tom by this time, and she saw that he was nodding his head and really meant yes.

She smiled at him and he winked at her with his winking eye, which was the left one, and then they went running off, with Battersea trotting and barking at their heels.

15

It wasn't very long before they found a clue. They were walking in single file around the edge of a field when Beth noticed something lying on the path.

"Wait!" she said, and stooped down to look more closely. It was a liquorice allsort, one of the round, pink coconut ones with a black centre. She picked it up and gave it to Tom.

"Thank you," he said. "One of my favourites!" He was about to put it in his mouth, but Beth stopped him just in time.

"Don't eat it!" she cried, snatching it back.

"Why not?" he said.

"For one thing it has been on the ground."

"Oh, I don't mind a little bit of dirt," he said. "I'm not fussy."

"And it's a clue! It's evidence. Father Christmas must have dropped it. Which means that he has been along this path. Come on—and keep your eyes open for more clues."

It was Battersea who found the next liquorice allsort. It was a square one, coloured red, white and black, and it had fallen in the grass beside the track. Battersea sniffed at it and opened his mouth, but Beth rescued the allsort before he could eat it.

"Another one!" she said.

"What a waste of good allsorts," Tom said. "There must be a hole in one of the boxes."

A little further on they came up against a problem, for they reached a sort of crossroads where one path went left, another one went right and, straight ahead, there lay a wood.

Which way to go?

It was Tom who solved the problem. He crouched down and examined the ground very carefully. After a few minutes, he straightened up.

"I think he went into the wood," he whispered.

"Why?" Beth whispered back.

"Look. The grass just on the edge has been pressed down by someone treading on it. And here, on this bush, one or two of the twigs are broken—he probably snapped them off as he brushed past."

"That's very good," Beth whispered, "very clever."

"Come on," Tom said, still in a whisper.

"Why are we whispering?" asked Beth.

"Sh-sh!" he hissed. "I don't think he can be very far away. We don't want him to know that we are on his trail."

They crept forward into the wood, looking for more clues. It was only a small wood and the trees were not very close together, so that there was lots of light. But, although they searched everywhere, all they found was something that looked like a footprint and they could not even be sure of that.

They stopped under a tree to think out what to do next. The tree was old and hollow but it still had some branches and, jumping up, Tom took hold of a low branch and began to swing.

"What are you doing?" asked Beth.

"I'm dreeping," said Tom.

"What on earth is dreeping?" asked Beth.

"Can't you see? This is dreeping." And he swung himself back and forth.

"We call it swinging," said Beth.

"That's not a very good word," said Tom. "Dreeping is much better. Come on, there's plenty of room. Have a dreep."

"We haven't time for that!" said Beth crossly; suddenly she pointed to the tree. "Look! Look!"

A door had opened in the trunk of the tree!

Tom stopped his dreeping and together they crept up to the door. They spotted at once that it was connected by some wire to the branch on which Tom had been swinging, so that when he pulled it down the door opened.

Beth put her head inside very carefully. At first, all she could see was blackness but slowly her eyes got used to it, and she saw a sort of tunnel sloping sharply downwards and curving, rather like a helter-skelter. Way, way below, at the bottom of the tunnel, she thought she could see a glimmer of light.

And she was sure that she could smell something also. It was faint but she was sure that she had smelt it before. What could it be?

Then, all at once, it came to her. Gorgonzola cheese! She could smell toasted cheese! What a strange smell to come from a tree!

She moved aside to let Tom have a look but, as she did so, Battersea, who had a weakness for Gorgonzola cheese—especially when it was toasted —jumped up and hurtled through the door. Beth put out a hand to stop him but she was too late.

Battersea went whooshing down the tunnel, as if he was on a slide, and within a second he had disappeared!

"Oh, my goodness!" cried Beth.

"I'll go in and get him," said Tom bravely.

"No," she said, "I ought to go. He is my dog."

"We'll both go," he said.

"Where does it lead?" she whispered.

"I don't know," he replied.

"Will we be able to get out?"

"I hope so," he said. "Tell you what. Give me your handkerchief."

"What for?"

"We'll tie it to the branch. The others will see it when they come looking and they will know where we are. And I'll prop the door open as well, to give them another clue."

"Good idea," said Beth.

She tied her handkerchief to the tree, while Tom dragged a fallen branch across and propped it against the door in such a way that it could not close.

"Right!" he said. "I'll go first. Keep close behind me."

Tom squeezed under the branch and through the door, followed by Beth. He sat down at the top of the sloping tunnel and she sat behind, holding him round the waist. It was really like sitting at the top of a slide in a playground, except that everything was so dark and eerie.

"Are you ready?" Tom whispered.

"Ready," Beth whispered.

"Right. Off we go then."

Tom pushed off with his feet and they went whistling away down the tunnel, their shoulders brushing the sides. They whooshed round a bend, going faster and faster and faster, and Beth clung to Tom even more tightly.

The tunnel went on and on and down and down, curving and bending and growing lighter as they sped along. Beth wondered if it would ever come to an end.

It did! Very suddenly! The slide came to a sharp

halt and they went hurtling over a ledge, and dropped with a great *boomp* on to a big heap of ferns.

The ferns were springy and soft so that they were not hurt at all, only a little shaken. Beth lay there for a moment trying to get her breath back and she felt something lick her face. She opened her eyes. It was Battersea! And he was all right!

"Oh, Battersea!" she cried.

She sat up, cuddling him in her arms, and then she saw a man with a white beard and white hair smiling down at her.

"Hello," he said. "I'm glad you dropped in."

Dropped in, thought Beth. She smiled to herself—that is exactly what she had done!

16

Of course, it was Father Christmas. He was not wearing his red coat and hat or his boots, just an old sweater and a pair of trousers with lots of pockets. But Beth had only to look at his face, with the snow-white beard and whiskers, and the kind, twinkling eyes, to know who he was.

"Hello, you young ragamuffin!" he said to Tom. "It took you long enough to find me." He held out his two hands, helped them to their feet, and gave Tom a big warm hug.

"How's your mother?" he asked.

"She is very cross with you!" Tom said.

"Bless my boots!" Father Christmas laughed. "In a bad mood, is she? Well, I'll soon jolly her out of that!"

Beth was looking round. They were in a sort of cave, but she could see at once that it was a very

131

special sort of place, more like an underground palace. Dozens of lanterns in bright colours hung from the roof, casting a warm and gentle glow. The walls looked like rock, but they were encrusted with hundreds of thousands of small glass-like objects that glowed and glinted in the light.

It was only when she drew nearer that Beth realised that these objects were sweets and toffees of all kinds—lemon and acid drops, buttermints, butter brazils, caramels, lollipops, fruit pastilles, glacier mints, fruit gums, humbugs, jelly beans, pear drops, wine gums, and lots of others. She had never seen so many, even in a sweet shop!

"How do you like my little hidey-hole?" asked Father Christmas.

"Terrific!" said Beth.

"It is my private place," said Father Christmas. "Everyone needs a place of their own, a secret place, don't you agree?"

"Yes, I suppose so," answered Beth.

"Of course it isn't secret any more. You and Tom know about it."

"Mother will be very umpty when she finds out," Tom said.

"Oh, she'll get over it," said Father Christmas. "She is never umpty for long."

Tom went across and tried to pull a buttermint from the wall.

"Hey!" roared Father Christmas, "that's enough of that! Leave the wall alone!"

"Can't I have just one?" pleaded Tom.

"No, you cannot! I'm not having you eat my walls! If you are hungry, you'll find some toasted cheese and sausage rolls down there."

He pointed to the end of the cave where there were some stools, a table, and a small barbecue. Now Beth realised where the smell of cheese had come from, for on top of the barbecue there were several slices of bread covered in golden-brown toasted cheese.

Tom began to eat immediately and Battersea sat at his feet, hoping for a morsel of toasted cheese, but Beth was too excited to join them. She had so many questions to ask Father Christmas, but she felt rather shy and hardly knew where to begin. Then she remembered the liquorice allsorts.

"We found these on the way here," she said, holding out the two allsorts. "I think they are yours."

"Blow my buttons!" he exclaimed. "Am I pleased to see those! Thank you, my dear. Just what I need for my Christmas card."

Beth looked puzzled. She could not imagine what liquorice allsorts could possibly have to do with Christmas cards.

Seeing her look, Father Christmas said: "Come over here and I'll show you."

He took her to the table and showed her a wooden tray which was packed with liquorice allsorts. They were arranged to make a picture just like a Christmas card, a picture of Kermit the Frog building a snowman. Underneath the allsorts formed the words MERRY CHRISTMAS.

Father Christmas pushed the two allsorts into one of the corners. "You don't happen to have any more allsorts on you, do you?"

"No. I'm sorry," said Beth.

"Pity," said Father Christmas. "I need one more boxful to finish the card."

"What will you do when it is finished?" asked Beth.

"I shall send it to myself next Christmas. I've always wanted a Christmas card that I could eat," he said with a chuckle.

"It won't be much of a Christmas," Beth said sadly, thinking of all those presents waiting in the Grotto.

"Oh, I don't know about that!" he said cheerfully, and he skipped across the floor to a swing that was suspended from the roof. He sat on the swing and said: "What is your name?"

"Beth," she replied.

"Well, don't look so sad, little Beth. Come and give me a push."

She gave him several pushes and he went swinging away, back and forth and higher and higher. Really, Beth thought, this is very odd. Walls made of sweets, a Christmas card you could eat and Father Christmas on a swing! Her friends would never believe her—if she ever told them, that is.

Father Christmas was smiling all over his face and it was obvious that he was enjoying himself no end.

"Do you want a turn?" he asked, when the swing finally slowed down and stopped.

"Not just now," she answered politely.

He went skipping off again towards a seesaw. "Come on," he called, "let's have a seesaw!"

Really Beth wanted to talk about next Christmas and about all the presents in the Grotto waiting to be wrapped, but Father Christmas didn't seem to want to talk about things like that.

"The main drawback of the seesaw," he said, "is that you can't work it on your own. You need at

least two people for a seesaw. So I am glad that you are here, Beth. I like seesawing. It is one of my weaknesses. But I haven't had a decent seesaw in ages."

It was no good at first, because Father Christmas was far too heavy and his end of the seesaw stayed down while Beth was stuck up in the air.

"Oh, blow my buttons!" said Father Christmas in irritation. And then he shouted: "Come on, Tom, lad! You are needed urgently."

"Coming!" said Tom, with a mouthful of toasted cheese.

Tom sat behind Beth and the extra weight just did the trick. The seesaw rocked up and down perfectly, and Father Christmas chuckled with pleasure. But he noticed that Beth looked thoughtful.

"Aren't you enjoying yourself?" he asked.

"Yes," said Beth, "I'm quite enjoying it." And then the questions all came out in a rush.

"What is going to happen next Christmas? Please, please tell me. I must know. Will all the presents in the Grotto be wrapped in time? Why did you stay in bed for all that time? What *is* going to happen, please?"

But, before he could answer, there was a

tremendous *boomp*, followed by another *boomp* and another, as Mother Christmas came flying out of the tunnel followed by Fred and then Bo.

Battersea started to bark with excitement and, without thinking, Beth and Tom got off their end of the seesaw. Father Christmas's end was in the air at this moment, but it came down suddenly and there was yet another *boomp* as he fell off, on his bottom.

17

In a moment, there was a real hullabaloo! Mother Christmas pulled herself up angrily and, picking up a stem of fern leaves, advanced on Father Christmas.

"So there you are, you old thingumajig!" she shouted. "You troublesome twit! You piffly old person! What do you mean by hiding down here! Do you know the trouble you have caused? What have you got to say for yourself, eh?"

She began to whack him across the shoulders with the ferns. They didn't really hurt, because the stem was thin and the leaves soft, but Father Christmas backed away.

"I can explain, my dear," he said.

"Explain! So I should think, you soppy old saucebox! You've got a lot of explaining to do! What about all those presents that are waiting to be wrapped? Answer me, answer me!"

But since she kept whacking him with the ferns, he didn't really have much chance to answer. He started to run and she chased after him, round and round the cave. Fred tried to stop her.

"Wait," he said.

"Out of my way," cried Mother Christmas, pushing him aside. "My dander is up!"

Beth felt quite sorry for Father Christmas, and wished that Mother Christmas's dander would soon go down.

Bo tried to help. "Wait, please," she said.

"Out of my way," cried Mother Christmas, swishing the ferns. "I intend to teach the old

fiddle-faddle a lesson!" And she chased after Father Christmas.

"Come here!" she shouted. "Come here, you great noodle! What do you mean by hiding away? We were worried sick!"

"Blow my buttons!" cried Father Christmas. "Let me get a word in edgeways."

"I'll word you!" she said, whacking out with the ferns. "I'll edgeways you!"

Father Christmas was growing desperate and breathless. Panting like a dog on a hot day, he leaped on to the swing.

"Help!" he called. "Help, or she will fern me to death!"

Beth gave the swing a push, just as Mother Christmas made a rush, and Father Christmas swung away out of reach. He was standing up on the seat of the swing, clinging to the ropes, and, each time he came swinging back, Mother Christmas whacked his legs with the ferns and shouted,

"Nincompoop! Noodle! Nitwit!"

"Do something, Tom!" said Beth.

But Tom was munching some more of the toasted cheese and seemed quite unconcerned. "Don't worry," he said. "She doesn't mean anything. It's a sort of game. She loves him really.

141

Anyway, she'll soon get tired."

And sure enough, after a few more minutes, Mother Christmas threw down the ferns and said, in a quiet voice: "All right. You can come down now."

She sat down on one of the stools and mopped her brow. "It's hard work chasing Father Christmas," she said, shaking her head.

Father Christmas looked down at her cautiously and kept on swinging. "Do you feel better, dear?" he asked.

"Much better," she said. "I must say, I am glad to see you safe and sound."

"If that's what you do when you are glad to see me, I wonder what you'd do if you were sorry to see me!" he said.

They both laughed at this, and Beth and Fred and Bo, pleased that the chasing was all over, began to laugh also. Battersea, who didn't like to be left out of anything, barked happily. Tom only smiled. He couldn't laugh because he was still eating the cheese.

Father Christmas came down and gave Mother Christmas a big hug. "I really am pleased you came, old dear," he said.

"Did I hurt you?" she asked.

142

"No, not at all. It would take more than a bunch of ferns to hurt me." He turned to Fred and Bo. "More visitors? You are very welcome."

"I am Beth's father," said Fred. "My name is Fred. It is an honour to meet you, sir."

"Bless my boots," said Father Christmas, "you don't have to call me sir. Father Christmas will do."

"And this is Bo who flies the helicopter," said Fred.

Bo smiled shyly. "I am pleased to meet," she said.

"Likewise," said Father Christmas. "Would you like a swing?"

"Not at the moment," said Bo.

"A seesaw? I'm very partial to the seesaw."

"Not just now," said Bo. "But I am thanking you."

"Another time, perhaps," said Father Christmas. "Would you like some toasted cheese?"

"There isn't any," Tom said, finishing the last piece.

"Oh," said Father Christmas. "Then I suggest we all go home and get something to eat there."

"That's easy to say but hard to do!" said Mother Christmas. "I can't crawl back up that tunnel!"

"You don't have to," replied Father Christmas. "There are some steps at the other end—and they lead right up to the trapdoor in our kitchen!"

"You cheeky beggar!" said Mother Christmas. "And you kept it a secret from me and Tom?"

"Well, I was working on a secret, wasn't I?" he said. "But it isn't really a secret any longer."

He went to a corner where something was hidden under a white sheet. Making a wide gesture like a magician about to take a rabbit out of a hat, he pulled the sheet away.

"Hey presto!" he said.

There, under the sheet, stood a very complicated but exciting-looking machine. Beth saw that there was a computer at the front, but she could not understand the part at the back. It had metal arms, and lots of big and little wheels and a metal platform.

"What on earth is it?" asked Mother Christmas.

"Can't you see?" said Father Christmas. "Does anyone in the assembled company know what it is?"

"I've seen something like it at the Post Office," said Fred, scratching his head with one hand and stroking his chin with the other. "Would it by any chance be a parcel-wrapping machine?"

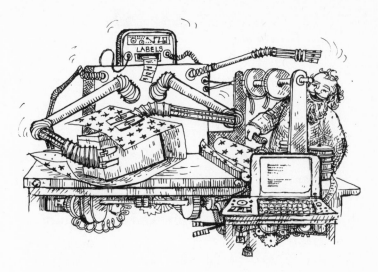

"Bingo!" cried Father Christmas. "A parcel-wrapping machine. The very latest thing!"

"Where did it come from?" asked Mother Christmas. "Did you spend our holiday money on this thing?" She looked as if she was about to get angry again.

"No, no, my old dear," he answered quickly. "I invented it and I made it."

"You!" she said.

"In person," he replied. "I finished it this morning. I decided that it was time to have some modern methods in the Grotto. It's such hard work wrapping all those parcels—especially for you and Tom. This computer will hold the names and addresses of all the children in the world, and will print them

145

on labels if necessary. We shan't have all the work of writing them out by hand any more. Look, I will give you a demonstration."

He turned to Beth. "What is your surname, Beth?"

"Hale," she said.

Father Christmas switched on the computer, then tapped some of the keys. There was a whirr and a hum, and Beth's name and address appeared on the screen.

"Beth Hale, 51 Shepherds Crescent, Kentish Town, London," said Father Christmas. "Is that correct?"

"Absolutely right!" said Fred.

"You clever old stick!" said Mother Christmas.

"Now I'll show you the wrapping-up bit," said Father Christmas. He put a cardboard box on the metal platform and pulled a lever. Almost at once, some brightly-coloured paper appeared, and the metal arms of the machine turned the box over and over until it was quite covered. Then the arms tucked in the folds and the box was all wrapped up.

"That took twelve seconds!" said Father Christmas. "Just think of the time we'll save. We shall be able to wrap and address the presents in the Grotto in a month instead of a year!" He smiled at Beth.

146

"So you don't have to worry any more, little Beth. Father Christmas will be round with his sack next Christmas as usual."

Beth smiled, but inside she felt quite guilty. She should have known that Father Christmas would never let the children down.

"I don't know how you found the time to make it," said Fred, "considering you spent over a month in bed!"

"Ha!" said Father Christmas. "I only spent the *days* in bed. At night I used to creep downstairs, go through the trap-door and come down here to work."

"You silly old sausage!" said Mother Christmas. "Why didn't you tell me and Tom about it?"

"It wouldn't have been a secret then, would it?" he answered. "And it wouldn't have been a surprise. You know how I like secrets and surprises."

He switched off the wrapping-up machine and skipped away towards the end of the cave.

"Come on," he cried, "let's go home. The last one to get there is a lemon!"

And they all rushed after him.

18

Mother Christmas wanted them to stay the night but Bo was anxious to fly the helicopter through the mountains before it got dark, so, after a quick tea, they had to go. Beth felt rather sad, but she cheered up when her father promised that they would all come back next year. That was something to look forward to!

They hugged each other and said goodbye at least six times. Tom gave Beth a present of a pen which she could hang round her neck with a piece of cord.

"Can I really keep it?" she asked.

"No," he said. But he nodded his head and winked, so that she knew it was all right.

Soon the helicopter rose into the sky. Beth saw Mother Christmas and Tom waving to her, but she couldn't see Father Christmas.

Then she did spot him. He had climbed on to the roof and he was standing on his head! He couldn't wave with his hands, so he waved at the helicopter with one leg.

In a few minutes the house was out of sight. Beth cuddled Battersea and sat back in her seat. What an adventure, she thought, I must write a poem about it. She started the poem in her head:

There's a house in a secret valley,
That is filled with magic and fun.
And Mother Christmas and Father Christmas,
Live there with Tom, their son.
Tom says 'yes' when he ought to say 'no',
And 'no' when he ought to say 'yes' . . .

Beth stopped there. She saw that Battersea was asleep in her lap and she suddenly felt very tired. She decided that she would finish the poem when they got home.

She closed her eyes, but only for a moment. Suddenly she was gripped by one of her feelings—a really strong feeling that the adventure was not over yet, and that something exciting was about to happen.

She sat up, wide awake now, and tried to puzzle out what it could be. Would they find Uncle Dan from Canada waiting for them when they reached home? No, that was unlikely, she thought.

Then she remembered that recently she had written an essay called *My Favourite Person* for a children's competition organised by the BBC. It was all about her father and she wanted to win (or at least be in the first five), not so much for the sake of the prize, but because she was truly proud of her dad and hoped that he would be proud of her.

But no, it wasn't that either. For she now had the feeling that what was about to happen would be bad. Exciting but bad. She felt a little tingle of apprehension run up her spine and prickle the back of her neck.

"I've got one of my feelings," she whispered to

her father, putting her mouth right up to his ear so that he could hear above the noise of the engine.

"What kind of feeling?"

"Something bad is going to happen."

"Hmph," he said. "I shouldn't worry about it. We're on our way home. Nothing much can happen now."

And that was all she could get out of him. She sat thinking about it for a while, and then the tiredness grew too much for her and she fell asleep.

19

It was snowing when they reached the little airport at Senja. Great flakes of snow, as big as two pence pieces, were falling from the grey sky so fast that they seemed to form a screen, making it impossible to see more than a few metres ahead. And there was a powerful wind too, which rocked the helicopter and hurled the giant snowflakes in gusts against the windows.

Beth was relieved when they landed safely near the airport terminal building. A snowplough had cleared a space for the helicopter and she could just see it at work nearby, shooting out great columns of snow as it moved along.

She wrapped Battersea's jacket around him and buttoned it up, then put on her red anorak and pulled up the hood. It was only a short distance to the terminal but, even so, they were covered in snow by the time they reached shelter.

"Phew," said Fred, "I'm chilled right through to the marrow of my bones."

"You will not be able to fly to Oslo today," said Bo. "The weather conditions are not good. I will arrange for you to stay at the hotel tonight, and you can your journey continue tomorrow. Please to wait here a moment."

Bo went down a corridor towards the Control Office where all pilots have to report before leaving or when arriving at an airport. She was carrying the envelope containing the map and the directions to Father Christmas's secret valley, which she had to hand back to Mr Andersen. Beth and Fred sat down and watched the snow swirling around outside.

"Do you fancy a sandwich—an open sandwich?" asked Fred, with a teasing smile.

But just as Beth was about to answer, Battersea interrupted her with a low, throaty growl.

"What's the matter?" she said, patting him. But he growled again, louder this time, and she saw that the hair just above his jacket collar was standing up. Then he squeezed himself under the wooden seat and lay with his chin on his front paws, watching a man who was hurrying towards them

153

along the corridor.

He looked like a pilot, for he was wearing a blue uniform with four rings of gold braid on each sleeve, and he was carrying an official-looking black case. As he went past them, with his head down, Battersea growled again and would have snapped at the pilot's ankles if Beth hadn't stopped him just in time.

"Down, Battersea!" she commanded. He settled down obediently, looking at her with big mournful eyes. It was obvious that he didn't think that he had done anything wrong.

Beth turned to apologise to the man, but he was already on his way to the exit.

"Not like Battersea to snap at people," said Fred, "not like him at all." He stood up, a puzzled look on his face, and sniffed the air. "Did you notice," he continued, "did you notice that when that pilot went by, the air suddenly felt cold and damp?"

"Yes!" said Beth excitedly. "Yes, I did."

They looked at each other for a moment and then, in the same breath, they both exclaimed:

"Mr Poley!"

"I wonder what mischief he has been up to," said Fred, with a smile.

Beth did not think that Mr Poley was a smiling matter, and she said: "Don't you think we should go after him?"

"He's gone," said Fred calmly. And, when Beth looked round, she could see that Mr Poley had disappeared through the exit doors.

"We would never find him in this weather," Fred said. "In any case, he probably had a car waiting and he will soon be miles away." He spoke quite happily, as if he didn't care a jot about Mr Roland Poley.

"But we must do something!" Beth said.

"What do you suggest?" asked Fred, still very calm.

"At least we should find Bo and warn her!" replied Beth in a sharp voice.

"All right. Let's do that," her father replied.

They set off down the corridor with Battersea at

their heels. Beth wanted to run but Fred refused to do anything but walk, even though she dragged at his arm and urged him to hurry. Really, she thought, her father could be quite infuriating at times.

They turned a corner into another corridor which was lined with offices. "She must be in one of these rooms," said Beth.

Now it was Battersea's turn to move into action. He began to scratch at one of the doors, whimpering and whining as he did so.

"It looks as if Battersea has found something," said Fred.

A strange sound came from within this room, as if someone was trying to talk through a pad of cotton wool or a pillow.

"Bo?" called Beth and waited.

Once again, they heard the strange muffled noise from within, and Battersea attacked the door even more fiercely.

"I don't like the sound of that!" Fred said, and he seemed more anxious now. The door was locked but he barged at it with his shoulder and it crashed open.

"Bo!" cried Beth, and rushed forward.

Bo was there all right, but she was lashed to a

chair with cord and could not move. She couldn't speak either because a thick woollen scarf had been tied tightly round her mouth.

"Mr Poley!" she gasped when Beth had untied the scarf. "Mr Poley! He has stolen the envelope with the map and the directions to the secret valley!"

"I said we should have gone after him!" Beth looked crossly at her father, but he was untying the cords and didn't seem to notice.

"He was disguised as a pilot," said Bo. "He came up behind me, took me by surprise."

"Are you all right?" asked Fred.

157

"Yes, yes, I am fine. But we must find that man. We must get the map and the papers back. Come, come!" said Bo urgently.

She moved to the door, but Fred simply plonked himself down on a corner of the table. "No hurry," he said.

"But he has the map!" cried Beth.

"No, he hasn't," said Fred.

"He took the envelope and put it in his case!" said Bo. "Please—hurry, hurry!"

"He may have put an envelope in his case," Fred said, "but he hasn't got the map or the directions."

"If he hasn't got them, who has?" asked Beth, feeling more and more bewildered by the minute.

"I have," said Fred, and, with a smile, he pulled the map and the papers from his inside pocket!

"Oh, this is wonderful!" cried Bo, and, to Fred's embarrassment, she gave him a hug and a kiss.

"Don't thank me," he said, backing away just in case Bo should try to kiss him again. "It was Beth who made me think of it."

"Me?" said Beth, in a puzzled voice.

"When we were on the helicopter. You told me that you had one of your feelings. Well, you are usually right, so I decided to take some simple

158

precautions. I took the envelope while you were
asleep and Bo was busy at the controls.''

"But what is in the envelope that Mr Poley has
taken?" asked Beth.

"Just some pieces of blank paper. On the top one
I wrote a little message for him.''

"A message?" asked Bo. "What kind of message?''

"Oh, I just wrote two words,'' Fred said.
"FOOLED AGAIN!''

Beth began to laugh as she imagined the look on
Mr Poley's face when he opened the envelope and
read the message. Bo began to laugh also and soon
Fred joined in, while Battersea, who didn't want to
be left out, barked too.

And that really was that. The secret of Father
Christmas was safe, at least until Mr Poley tried
again. And in the morning, when the weather
had cleared and they had said goodbye to Bo,
Fred, Beth and Battersea continued their journey
home.

"Well," said Fred, as the plane circled above
London Airport, "have you enjoyed yourself,
clever-socks?''

"Oh, yes!" said Beth.

"Which bit did you like best?" he asked.

Beth put her head on one side and thought for a moment. "Oh, I couldn't say," she answered. "I think I liked it all."